THE BOXER'S SOLILOQUY

THE BOXER'S SOLILOQUY

BY MATT LUCAS

Copyright © Matt Lucas, 2014
All rights reserved.
Printed by CreateSpace

ISBN 978-0-692-21143-4

The is a work of fiction. Names, characters, places, and incidents either are the product of the author's imagination or are used factiously, and any resemblance to actual persons, living or dead, business establishments, events, or locales is entirely coincidental.

The story "The Boxer's Soliloquy" was originally published in Spry Literary Magazine in the inaugural issue of December 2012. It can be viewed at www.sprylit.com

Designed by Lee Hunter
The typefaces used are Minion Pro and Futura LT.

DEDICATED TO

The boxers who win,
To the boxers who lose,
Most of all to the boxers
That continue to fight.

Table of Contents

Preface

Muay Thai is a ring sport originating in Thailand. Similar to Western boxing, each round in a professional bout is composed of three minutes with a two-minute break in between rounds. Unlike its Western cousin, Muay Thai bouts are only five rounds, during which the boxers may kick, punch, elbow, and knee each other.

The bouts in Thailand are scored based on a 10-9 point system. A boxer who wins the round will receive a 10, the loser a 9. The first few rounds are generally scored evenly and more weight is given to attacks that unbalance, damage, and faze the boxers. Additionally, the judges will favor the fighter who ends the fight stronger.

The Long Train Ride

"Where you go?"

A Thai woman stood before us when we arrived at Hua Lamphong train station. The large building was decorative compared to the surrounding structures that somehow survived the daily apocalypse of pollution. The building was a drab white, its color marred by the soot from the Bangkok atmosphere. The roof was gilded in royal yellow, giving it a monarchist appeal.

"Ayutthaya."

I looked away from the Thai woman and at her. She was dressed in black tights, Toms, and a t-shirt with extended armholes. Her shirt had a cat holding an electronic piano/guitar and the words "Save the world play my keytar."

I went to grasp her hand and fell short of my mark. I was in constant search of her hand: when we crossed the traffic-ridden streets of the metropolis, when we walked along the beaches, when we sat in the bars on Khao San Road and watched the other backpackers, drunk off cheap alcohol and travel, traverse through the herd of streetside sellers.

"Okay, you go there."

The Thai woman pointed us toward a line of people who were buying tickets. We bought two tickets for thirty *baht* total. Our train was to leave in thirty minutes. We took a seat in the red chairs that lined the lobby. Across from us a mother and child talked to each other. I wondered what they said.

"I'm going to the bathroom."

I nodded and absently watched her walk to the restrooms. She hated the bathrooms of Thailand.

"I can get used to anything, but the lack of toilet paper is really far too much for me."

She brought a roll of toilet paper everywhere we went. She complained about her mosquito bites when she came back.

The large clock hands showed eleven a.m. I took her hand.

"Let's go get on the train."

We rose and walked to the platform. There were three trains on the six lines. I showed my ticket to a worker and she pointed to the far end. The train was yellow. Perhaps once it was gold but years of smog and use had sullied it. The black soot and the black machinery of the train gave it the look of a dirty bumblebee; a long, foul insect.

We got on and sat opposite each other by the window. The seats were made of a cheap polished wood. My eyes scanned over them for the signs of knife-scrawled graffiti but found none. The window was open and a train, jaundiced and unclean like our own, obstructed the view outside.

The engine began with a whir. The train lurched forward. As the wheels churned, the coal-driven machine trudged along.

She pointed outside.

"Bangkok is dirty."

"Parts of it." I followed her fingers to where she was pointing.

"Most of it."

I looked back out the window. The landscape was moving along at a steady pace, in time with the heavy machinery of the locomotive. We passed by a small *khlong*, the water in the canal was brown with sediment. A few ramshackle shacks, devoid of charm, stood by the water. The roofs were corrugated tin. The sun struck through gaps in the metal.

A small boy came out of a shack, followed by another boy who was even younger. The smaller boy waved at the train while the older stared blankly. She looked at me.

"Is this what all of Thailand is like?"

"Parts of it."

"So most of it?"

"No, just parts."

She leaned back, opened her bag and rummaged through it. She'd bought it in Khao San. The bag was cloth and embroidered. The front had an ornate design of an elephant. Its tusks were long and made of a silvery thread. The cloth was red and the country's beast of burden was highlighted by the contrast between thread and material. She began to dig through it.

"Sooo…"

"So what?"

"So how was it, dummy?"

"I don't know. Painful. Fun. Tough. Now it's over."

"You're sooo stoic."

"Whatever."

"Well, did you get paid a lot?"

"Not really, I made 1,500 *baht* for the fight."

"That's what, like fifty dollars?"

"Yeah, not really that much."

"How long were you here for?"

"A month."

"How much did you train?"

"About six or seven hours a day. I'd run twice a day, hit pads, clinch, spar every day, then a lot of sit ups and push ups."

"Was it worth it?"

"I guess so."

"You don't know, or you haven't decided?"

"Decided what?"

"Decided if it was worth it or not."

"I came out here to fight."

"So it was worth it?"

"Well I did what I came for."

"How long will it take to get there?"

"About an hour and a half."

She rummaged for a few more minutes and took out her iPhone. She put in her earbuds, silencing the steady rhythm of the movement on the tracks in favor of American pop music.

She looked at her watch.

"We're almost halfway there."

I nodded.

"So my guidebook said that Ayutthaya used to be the capital of Thailand, back when it was called Siam."

I looked at my hand. My index knuckle was cut. The wrappings hadn't provided enough protection, nor had the boxing gloves. The skin had peeled off my knuckle as I threw a right cross during the fight. I remembered the bitter sting of sweat and the grime of the glove mixing with my small laceration. The wound hurt for only a moment, then the pain passed, replaced by more poignant injuries.

"Then the Burmese sacked it and the capital moved down to Bangkok. First the capital was on the western side of the Chao Phraya River, but gradually things moved to the other side. Maybe we should have taken a boat ride down the river."

"We'll take a ferry across the river to Ayutthaya."

"Oh, that will be fun."

"Suppose so."

The train lazily shook side to side. A woman walked slowly down the aisle with an assortment of drinks in an ice-filled bucket: water, a can of Leo beer, and several plastic bottles of Coke.

"Water, water, Leo." She pointed at her wares.

Her skin was dark from the sun. Her flat nose bespoke her Isaan origins.

"Drink, drink, want drink?"

The combination of ice, cans, and bottles rattled as she walked by.

I looked out the window and then set my head against the side of the train. My head rocked side to side with the locomotive. My eyes shut and I fell asleep.

In my dream her plane arrived a few days before my fight—not a few days after, as it actually happened, so she was there when I was in the ring. The bell sounded, ending the last of the five rounds. I'd trained for so long, here in Thailand and at home. I'd saved so much money and worked so hard to be here. She had come. I got out of the ring and she came to me.

"You are so strong."

She laughed, an imaginary laugh. A motion I had never seen before, she leaned back and opened her mouth widely.

"I love you for what you do, no matter what it is you do."

Her lips met mine and I could feel her slide her hand down my arm and into mine.

◆◆◆

She kicked at my leg and I woke.

"Bryan, I think we're there. Everyone is getting off."

I nodded and rose. A large sign that said "Ayutthaya" showed we had arrived at our destination. We walked over a set of train tracks into the station. It was far less impressive than Bangkok's. The wooden benches were full of yellow-robed men. Their heads and eyebrows were shaved. I pointed at the men.

"See, monks."

"I don't think I've seen any monks since I've been here. Not even at Wat Po. I wonder what they're doing."

"Waiting for the next train."

"Of course, I meant where are they going? Why do you have to be so literal?"

I answered with silence. We walked through the train station. Down the steps was a line of *tuk-tuks* and *samlor* drivers.

"Where you go? Where you go?"

A Thai man stood near the train station; his nose was flat and his features wide. "You want map? Free. Free. Come, come."

He beckoned us with his hands and we followed him to the side of the train station where we had initially departed. In front of us was a large map of Ayutthaya with a star stating where we were. The former capital was not large and was surrounded on all sides by waterways. The rivers provided transport from the northern areas of Siam south to the trade center. Ayutthaya had had a rich market.

"You visit *Wat*? Come I show you."

He pointed back towards his *tuk-tuk*. I looked at his three-wheeled vehicle.

"How much?"

"Five hundred *baht*."

I turned away from the man and walked towards the boat.

"Let's take the ferry."

I reached for her hand. She put it in mine gingerly. We walked back towards the *tuk-tuks*.

"Four hundred!"

The Thai man's hands were cupped around his mouth.

"Four hundred *baht*, that's only like thirteen dollars."

Her mind was full of calculations.

"I want to ride bikes."

"It's so hot out."

"It will be fun."

"It's so hot out."

She let go of my hand. We walked toward the water. A woman sat at a desk. On the metallic counter was a small sign saying that the ferry would be four *baht*. I paid the woman with a ten-*baht* coin. She gave me change. We walked down a small ramp to the dock. It bobbed up and down with our weight when we stepped on it. A young woman was on the dock already, clad in a short black skirt and a white button-up blouse. I stared at her while the ferry came. The skirt was flattering, and she wore heels that made her legs shapely.

The ferry pulled up next to the dock and the passengers from the other side stepped off the motorized wooden contraption. We got on the boat. The driver swung the boat around lazily. We putted across the brown river. I looked into the water. It was murky and full of sediment. I thought of all the motorboats on the river that had turned the water to a shit brown. I looked at her and considered commenting on it. I stayed silent. We got off the boat on a similar dock and walked up a ramp. A line of shops offered motorbikes, bicycles, and food.

"Bicycles, bicycles, bicycles."

A white man stood inside the first shop. I walked up to him.

"Two."

I felt her pinch my side.

"No problem. I just need a form of ID from you and eighty *baht*."

I handed over my American driver's license to him along with a hundred *baht* note. He took it and pointed at two bikes.

"Those two should fit you."

He called over to a man near him in Thai and the man came to him with a lock and two ten-*baht* coins. He handed the items over along with a photocopied map.

"These are the main *Wats* here. The laying Buddha is here, and there's a neat underground aspect to this *Wat* here. We ask you that you don't leave the island with the bikes as its much too far for you to come back."

"Thanks."

I nodded and I showed her the map. The bikes were large and clunky with odd stands that I'd never seen before. They were single-speed, each with a bell attached to the front. I rang the bell several times and she looked at me with annoyance. The lock was a thin chain covered in plastic—someone could cut through it with a sharp pair of scissors. The man went back inside of his small restaurant-shop and we walked our bikes to the end of the street.

"How am I supposed to carry my bag and ride a bicycle?"

"You want me to carry it?"

"No, I'll do it."

"Well then."

I got on my bike and pushed off. The first street was busy with traffic and it took a moment to get on the correct side of the road.

"That was scary. I can't seem to get which side we should be on and how turns work."

Her voice faded in and out with the noise of passing cars.

"I remember reading a book about a man who goes from Japan to Hawaii all the time. The traffic goes in different directions, and when he got back to Hawaii he crossed the street but he looked the wrong way because he thought he was back in Japan. He got hit by a car and died."

"Oh."

"So where should we go first?"

"If we make a loop around the center of the island we should be able to see most of the *Wats*."

We rode our bikes three or four miles down a paved road. A few cars and a handful of *tuk-tuks* passed us. The road signs were unintelligible. I stopped repeatedly to check that we were going the right way. Eventually I saw ruins in the distance.

"Let's stop there."

"Which one?"

"The one on the left."

She rang her bell. We rode to the far end of the ruined area and then took our bikes off the road and onto the grass-patched dirt. A few monks sat on one of the brick remains. Their seats were covered by the shade of a lone tree. They looked at us silently as we rode past. She rang her bell.

We made our way to the main entrance and locked our bikes to a post. A small stand was set up by the entrance selling tickets and offering brochures and audio tours.

I paid 100 *baht* for our passes.

"It's free for Thais I think."

I looked at the stand. She reached towards it.

"I want to get a brochure too."

We walked into the former temple. A waist-high brick wall enclosed the grounds. The red bricks had turned pink from exposure to the sun.

"This is Wat Chai Wattanaram. The temple symbolized the pinnacle of art during the Ayutthaya period, according to the brochure. I'm really glad that I brought my camera. This is beautiful."

The crab grass was a mix of dull green and straw brown from lack of water. I walked slowly on the lawn, my thigh occasionally stinging with pain. The skin had become jaundiced from getting leg-kicked during the fight, causing me to walk with a limp.

She hurried on before me, walking through the various structures. Several tops of the two-story towers were conical while others spiraled towards the sky. The latter looked as if they would penetrate the heavens.

"Will you take a picture of me?"

"Of course."

She sat down on the stairs of a structure whose conical top was still intact. I took the camera from her bag.

"The Burmese sacked Ayutthaya in 1767, destroying the city. I guess this is what is left."

The sun hit her face, warming it. My skin was getting hot. I wanted water.

"So what have you been doing the last few days before I came in?"

"Nothing. I stayed at the camp. I got the room in Khao San the day before you came. I rested."

"You didn't go out and see anything?"

"I was tired."

"You've never been to Thailand before. There's so much to see."

She swept her hand around, brooming the clouds.

"I can't believe you didn't go anywhere."

"I went around Bangkok a little."

"Oh yeah?"

"Yeah. I went out with this Swedish guy that I met on Khao San."

"Was it fun?"

"I suppose so."

"You're not sure?"

"No, I'm not sure."

"Well, why not?"

I didn't answer her and kept walking. Across the street was another temple.

"Want to go to that temple there?"

My feet were already in the road. She trailed along.

"Sure."

We walked towards the entrance.

"Look at the headless Buddhas. It's so sad that something so beautiful could be destroyed so easily. You'd never do something like that would you?"

"I suppose not."

"But you're not sure?"

"No I'm not sure."

"Well why would you ever do something like that?"

"If I was in a different place, at a different time, I might be a different person, and I might do something like that."

"I'm not sure I believe that. We are who we are, good or bad."

I nodded and we walked to our bikes. I looked at her hand as it rested on the bike handle. Her fingernails were manicured, with no dirt underneath them. Her hands had a softness to them. I put my hand on hers.

She looked at me quizzically. I took my hand off hers and mounted the bike. I began to pedal away. We rode back across the grass and dirt then crossed the street to Wat Mahat. A *tuk-tuk* sat outside of the temple grounds waiting for its passengers. The driver sat under a nearby tree smoking a cigarette. The entry stand to the temple priced entry at fifty *baht* per person for *farang*. It was free for Thais.

We walked into the grounds. We entered a large hallway that was uncovered.

She ran her fingers along the wall. Her hand pushed into a gap in the structure.

"Look, a window."

While the roof of the hall was absent, the supporting walls were intact. The builders had made large open holes, windows for the brick walls. I looked out of them onto the rest of the grounds. I saw more brick buildings, more grass, and a few trees.

"This place is so beautiful. My guidebook says that this temple was one of the spiritual centers of the city. Do you think that's why there are so many Buddha statues?"

"All the statues are missing their heads."

"It probably happened when the Burmese sacked the town."

"Probably."

"Who was that Swedish guy that you met?"

"Oh, just this guy. He was in the same hostel."

"Where did you go?"

"Um, just around Bangkok."

She turned and faced me. Her arms hung akimbo.

"You don't remember where you went?"

"I sort of do."

"Did you get drunk?"

"A little."

"So you went to a bar?"

"Yeah, I guess so."

"It was a bar or it wasn't a bar?"

I sighed. I put my hands in my pockets. I was getting annoyed.

"They served alcohol."

"Did they serve food?"

"No."

"So it was a bar?"

"Yeah, I guess a lot of the people there were drinking."

She walked a few feet away. The sun was getting hotter. I could see the sweat condensing on her brow. I wished I had brought water.

"You went to a whorehouse!"

"I'd never been before."

"And you never should have gone. Those women are exploited."

"What makes them any different from anyone else?"

"They have to sell their bodies for a living!"

"And…"

"You disgust me."

The sun seemed to be getting even hotter. I walked up to her.

"Get away from me."

"You've been saying that for a long time."

Her eyes went hard.

"What's that supposed to mean?"

I felt exasperated. My shoulders felt tense, welled up.

"When did you last care? You didn't even come to my fight."

"I had to work."

"You came out here for a week, and you couldn't come out three days earlier?"

"I told you I had to work."

"You always have to work, or you're always tired, or you always have a headache."

"You're changing the subject."

"No, I'm not."

The temple grounds appeared even more ruined, as if the last bit of history had been sacked. The bricks were worn by the sun. The color that was once brilliant had been washed out by daily rays.

She turned away from me.

"I want to leave."

"Okay, go."

"Fine, fuck you, you fucking whoremongering asshole."

"She was a better fuck than you anyways."

My words spat spite onto the ground. I watched her walk away. I could see the sweat running down the back of her arms into her palms. Her hands would have been scalding. Her bag swung like a pendulum from her shoulder. I walked over to a tree and sat down. I waited there, watching the sun move from east to west. The air slowly grew colder. I got up and went to the bikes. Hers was gone. I took the ferry back to the train station and waited for the last train of the evening. It got off to a slow start as it moved from the former capital back to Bangkok.

•••

"Please stand clear of the closing doors."

The train doors closed. She and her girlfriend were dressed for the evening. They were seated next to each other. They had gone out. Her elephant-embroidered bag sat next to her. She didn't know why she'd taken it out tonight, nor why she took it out so often. Its glittery thread was worn and it no longer held its exotic appeal to her yet she still carried it with her.

Her girlfriend shifted on the train seat and her lips curled into an old lemon rind.

"I wish we had taken a cab."

"I'd rather take the trains."

"Why? Because you're cheap? Like your bag?"

"No. It's something about train rides."

"Well, what about them? And why didn't you go back with that guy? If you had I wouldn't have to be riding this damn train. It's so filthy."

"He was okay, he just didn't seem that classy."

"Classy? You want someone that's classy? God, how long has it been since Thailand?

"I don't know."

"What do you mean you don't know? Ugh, you know we're riding the train? The subway is so dirty."

"I like trains, they remind me of being a different person at a different time."

Abby

I hated them.

The building next to mine was an old Victorian. A horde of twenty-somethings lived there. The house was a constant din of comings and goings.

It was a beehive of idiots. I had nicknames for the six inhabitants that resided there for that one irritating year. The one with the red hair was Queen Bee, and her boyfriend was Drone Number 1. Another woman was The Mediocre Mare. I mused about how many times she visited the clinic for clap medication, considering the hordes of bestial men that came to see her, no doubt dates from Craigslist. The other three boys were identical; one shitbag looked the same as another. I just titled them by number: 2, 3, and 4. Without them, though, Abby would never have come into my life. That's why I hate them so much now.

I was sitting on my balcony one evening when I heard them speak. They'd been in the building next door for ten months. I desperately prayed that their lease would be up. My hopes were for a nice geriatric couple to take over so that I might get a night of sleep without marijuana smoke wafting over to my apartment. Most of the time I was able to ignore their inane dialogues but I ended up eavesdropping.

The Queen Bee stood on the porch with a joint in her mouth trying to keep the smoking stick away from Drone Number 1. The drone stood with his mouth agape.

"Do you know how LSD was invented?"

Queen Bee stared at Drone Number 1 as if he had no pollen to give to the hive.

"Didn't it have to do with some guy in the CIA?"

"Yeah, they were attempting to create a truth serum to use on prisoners of war. This guy Albert Hofmann created LSD and took a big hit of it one day while he was riding his bicycle."

"Wow, I didn't know that. What happened?"

"Well, obviously it exploded his consciousness. He started to realize how vast the fucking universe really is. He tripped balls. He started taking it all the time."

"Did the truth serum idea ever work out?"

"I don't think so. Do you know where we can score any? Do your coworkers have some?"

"I don't know, let me call Nick."

A few minutes later the Drone resumed the conversation.

"Nick doesn't have any acid but he did find a dog."

"A dog?"

"Yeah, isn't that sweet?"

"Next time Nick comes by he should bring the dog."

"We can get the dog high."

They laughed and I went back inside. The evening had been spoiled by my foolishness in listening to those assholes.

A few weeks passed and I began to see more of Nick and more of the dog. The dog was a small brown and white pit bull mutt. She ran rampant in the streets as Nick smoked pot with my neighbors. When the dog was tired from scurrying about the street she would sleep on the stoop of my apartment. I began to leave small bits of food and kept a small bowl of water for her. After a month Nick replaced Drone Number 1 in Queen Bee's hive and the dog was a live-in resident. The mutt was ignored and left to her own devices.

•••

I worked late nights as a bartender at a local dive. The bar was in the east part of town and most of the clientele were local drunks. They kept me serving until the end of the night. I would take a late-night bus back home and I would see the dog sitting outside, usually on my stoop. After seeing her out there for a week I bought her one of those dog pillows. My attention to her, while initially out of a sense of duty, turned into a desire for companionship.

She seemed a little happier when I was with her. I bought a leash and would take her on late-night walks after work. We would walk to the waterfront park and I'd let her off the leash to run by the water. She'd run for a few minutes then mellow out and walk next to me as I followed the water line. It was on one of those walks when I named her. I called her Abigail, Abby for short.

I decided that my neighbors wouldn't notice her disappearance so I let her into my apartment when I got home from work one night. I started feeding her regularly and she filled out. Her coat started to shine. It was two weeks before I overheard my neighbors talking to each other about her vanishing.

I decided to move. The new place was a few streets away and the rent was a little higher, but I could keep Abby and not worry about my neighbors finding her. I didn't have much besides my job going for me, and I didn't much care about that. When I was home I felt like I had someone to talk to, though she couldn't talk back, but there was a way in which I felt she really listened to me.

I started taking Abby to the bar with me. That meant leaving for work earlier and coming home a bit later, but I didn't mind it. I didn't want her staying at home alone. It took about forty minutes to walk to work and she made me feel safe walking down the streets late at night, although truthfully she was a coward. When an unknown drunk would bend over to pet her at the bar she'd scuttle away.

It was a Thursday night at the bar and Frank was sitting in front of me. Frank had been coming in regularly for the last few months. He was a former straight edge vegan kid. He began to eat meat and was an incorrigible alcoholic. I didn't cut him off ever. If he knew how to control himself from drinking when he was straight edge, he should have been able to when at the bar. He started babbling to me about his bicycle and then his cell phone.

"Look at this new cell phone. I can get the Internet on it, I can text, I can take pictures…"

He became absorbed in his phone. He pushed his meaty fingers on the screen and then took a slug of his beer.

"How much does it cost?"

I was bored and it was another 15 minutes until last call.

"The phone was $150, then the service is $60 a month."

"Oh."

I thought momentarily about acquiring a cell phone then decided once more against it. I got one for two months but no one ever called. The lack of calls just made me depressed. I would look at the phone and wait for it to ring. I would think about all the people walking downtown gabbing away endlessly on their phones and then my phone, dead, silent. I switched back to a landline and hooked my answering machine to it. I got the same amount of telephone calls, which is to say, none. Well, sometimes a telemarketer left a message.

"Where's Abby?"

"She's over here."

I pointed at her lying at the end of the bar. Frank got up from his bar stool and wobbled over towards her. Abby hated Frank. Frank had a mustache and Abby hated men with facial hair. She'd nipped at Frank a few times, but when Frank got drunk he always tried to pet her.

"You should probably leave her alone."

I wouldn't do anything to Abby if she bit him. Frank didn't tip well and he was a loser. It's one thing to be a loser, it's quite another to be a loser who doesn't tip. I'd probably let Abby rip his intestines out and be halfway through digesting his liver before I bothered calling 911.

Frank continued to stagger towards Abby, despite my warnings and their past relationship.

"Here doggy, come here doggy."

Frank clapped his fingers together. He looked like an ape, a particularly stupid and drunk ape. Abby started growling, as he got closer.

"Come on, come on."

Abby's growling got louder as Frank's sausage fingers came at her.

"Frank, she's growling. She's going to bite you and it's going to be your fault."

Frank didn't listen to me and inched his fingers closer to Abby's face. Her teeth were bared and she lashed out at Frank's hand. She bit hard, drawing blood. She scuttled back behind the bar and knocked into my leg. Frank let out a howl that was followed by laughter from the other patrons. Most of the regulars had seen this scene acted out before, and it still had a comical appeal to them. Frank pulled his fingers into his mouth and began to suck on them.

"She bit me! Simon, your dog bit me!"

His voice was garbled as his tongue lay between his fingers.

"She always does. You need to keep your mitts away from her. She bites you every time. She doesn't like you."

"I'll have a shot of JD."

I nodded and poured him his drink.

"Last call."

A few patrons got more drinks but most of them were either plastered already or too poor to buy another. They sulked in their seats for another ten minutes before I announced closing time.

The drunks shuffled out, ushered by my lackadaisical arm waving. They knew the routine. The smart ones had already left a few minutes ago to walk to the liquor store. They'd buy some malt liquor, a fifth of vodka, or maybe some Bacardi Breezers that they'd spike with rum to keep them going until their eyes closed or their livers gave out.

It took about fifteen minutes to close up the bar. I

counted my money before I left. It was a slow night. The money had never mattered to me. Even with taking care of Abby I still had plenty of money. I would buy her dog pillows, endless amounts of biscuits, bones, and squeaky toys. She'd gnaw at the annoying squeaky balls that I got her for a day and then discard them, totally uninterested. She liked to spend most of her time lying by my feet while I sat on my recliner watching TV. She was a lazy dog.

"Come on Abby."

I shut off the lights. She came up from her position at the end of the bar and walked to the door. She wagged her tail. I bent down and patted her head. I pushed in the code for the alarm, and let myself out. Abby followed. I locked the door from the outside and we started up the street. I didn't bother leashing her. This late at night there were only a few crackheads around, whom we'd both avoid, and she was pretty good about not hopping into the middle of the street. We made it home. I checked the messages on my answering machine. There was one from a telemarketer. I listened the whole way through. I got a bottle of cola from my fridge, filled Abby's bowl with water, and sat down on the recliner. I stared off in the distance for a while then flipped on the tube to watch the old Cotto and Margarito fight.

Cotto was a fast, technical fighter. The first few rounds he dominated the less savvy Margarito. Cotto bobbed, weaved, and threw a variety of uppercuts into the taller boxer's mug. Margarito had a look of determination on his face as he repeatedly pushed Cotto up against the ropes, throwing straight punches relentlessly.

Most bouts the boys aren't boxing the whole time. They're sizing each other up, they're dancing about, they're waiting and picking their placement. This bout was a never-ending push and Margarito kept pushing, like Sisyphus pushing that rock up the hill although Margarito's efforts weren't in vain. He won the bout with his determination, not with his skill. Everyone knew that Cotto was a better boxer, but Margarito had the legs and the heart. That's what mattered. I watched the after-bout report and drank some water.

It was four o'clock. The sun would start to rise soon, I thought. I went and lay down in my bed. I patted the blankets and Abby hopped up next to me. She sniffed at my face and walked around on the mattress. She settled at the bottom, where she fell asleep. I could hear her light snores as I stared up at the ceiling. I thought of the boxers, about Frank's bloody fingers, and about Abby. My eyes drooped and I fell into a dreamless slumber.

Abby woke me up around noon. She had to piss. I hauled my body out of bed and put on my slippers. We walked outside and she urinated on the small patch of lawn out front. We strolled around the block and she dumped on a lawyer's lawn. I didn't bother picking up the crap. We went back to the house and I fed her. She got dry food in the mornings and then a mix of wet and dry at night. Sometimes I'd pick up a steak for her and feed it to her. It was a Jack London story that compelled me to buy her a piece of meat whenever I looked at my bookshelf. London wrote about an old boxer who fought a young guy. It was an age versus youth story. The old boxer tried to hold out but he didn't have the wherewithal. He didn't have the energy because he hadn't eaten well, he hadn't eaten his steak. I wanted to make sure that Abby would have the constitution if she ever needed it, so I fed her steak.

I ate cereal for breakfast and sat on the recliner. I watched the noon news and looked at the weather channel for a bit. After a few hours of sitting on my duff I took Abby out for a walk. We were strolling around for a bit when she caught sight of a cat. Abby didn't care about felines but this was the neighborhood tom. The cat pissed her off good. He'd sit and wait for Abby to come out for her morning moment of relief and would take a cheap swipe at her face then run off. Abby was always too confused to do much about it. When Abby saw the cat, she ran off. She broke her leash, which was a flimsy piece of twine, and went like Margarito after Cotto.

She almost had him, just like the taller boxer-the one with the heart and the legs-had the smaller boxer. She was three-fourths of the way through the intersection when the blue Subaru clipped her. She fell with a whine to the sidewalk. She was breathing heavily. Her chest heaved. Blood poured out from her back quarters. It looked like her ribs had gotten crushed. She whimpered for a moment and that was it. I closed her eyes and picked her up. The Subaru hadn't stopped and was long gone. I carried her back to my apartment and set her down on her dog pillow. I looked at her for two hours. The clothes I was wearing had blood on them so I threw them in the laundry and showered for work. I let the warm water hit my body. I hoped that the water would wash away my skin, like a snake or a grashopper. With a new skin maybe I'd be a new person. My skin didn't come off. I walked to work in a daze.

Work passed. It was like being half awake. Somewhere between sleep and wakefulness, where the sounds of the world come through and you reply but your mind isn't focused. My mind was still lost in the fog of sleep.

I walked back home. Abby's body made the apartment stink. The smell was like wet dog but worse. I got a few blankets together and wrapped her in them. I tied the blankets with some twine, left over from when I'd made her leash. I carried her to the park by the water. It was still dark out when I got to the bridge over the highway. The bridge overlooked a bit of water that sat next to the park. I stood on the bridge and looked out towards the bay. I could see the lights of the nearby bridge. I looked west and saw the lights of the city. They were bright against the darkness of the water. I set Abby's body down and thought about how she came into my life. I hated my old neighbors for my loss. They were to blame. Without them I would have never had her.

I picked up her body and swung it back and forth a few times to get a feeling of her weight. Time turned to gel. I let her body go. It sailed forward. The corpse hit the water. It made a small splash. I looked down. Her body sank. I walked home. Alone.

The Big Payday

He shuffled the money in his hands. The dollars were worn from numerous exchanges. He separated them by denomination and proceeded to count out the currency. He tallied his total and jotted it down on a scratch pad. He looked up his total sales, the food sales, and the bar sales, and deducted the tip outs for the other employees. The calculations ran quickly through his head. He would have a little more than a grand for his trip.

"Bryan, just give Sam your drop when you're done, and good luck, buddy. Kill 'em!"

James, the restaurant manager clapped his hand on Bryan's shoulder and kept walking. If he stayed at the restaurant he would probably get a position as a manager which meant more money, longer hours, not as much training. He would have to cut down on his boxing, and wouldn't be able to fight as much or at all.

"How did you do Bryan?"

Tanya sat counting out money.

"Pretty good, I'm walking with one hundred and fifty. I sold eleven hundred dollars worth of shit. What about you?"

"I sold a little more, thirteen hundred. I made two hundred dollars."

"You must have gotten some really good customers."

Bryan portioned out his tip outs and wrapped them in paper to be counted by the managers later with the rest of his cash drop. He stuffed everything into an envelope.

"Yeah, everyone seemed really nice. I've really gotten the hang of working here." She smoothed her skirt and sat straight in her chair.

"What's your plan, Bryan? You leave really soon for Thailand right? Today, or tomorrow…?"

"My flight is at one in the morning. I have to leave later this evening."

He leaned back in his chair and looked at Tanya.

She smiled at him.

"You must be excited. Have you saved enough money? Will they let you come back to work here when you return?"

"As long as I don't go too wild over there I should be okay. I guess I'm excited, a little nervous, too, to be honest. I've never been out of the country before."

"I went on a study abroad while I was in college. It was pretty amazing. After the semester was over I travelled all over Europe. I've never been to Asia before. I heard that Thailand has really beautiful beaches."

"Yeah that's what I heard. I've never been there. We'll see what happens. What about you? What's your plan?"

"I'll keep working here for a while. It's comfortable and I can move up. I feel like with the economy being like it is, it makes sense to stick it out here and advance. I can use my experience here plus my business degree to land something better later…Bryan, why are you going? I don't get it."

Bryan sighed.

"To train, to fight."

"Can't you train here? Aren't there gyms? Why do you have to fight?"

"I don't have to fight."

"So you want to?"

Bryan hesitated then spoke clearly.

"Yes."

"But you could get hurt. Don't boxers get brain damage? And then what? After you've fought? What do you get? A beaten body? Do you even get paid that much?"

Tanya put the money from her day's labor into her purse. Bryan left his out and counted it again.

"Tanya what do you get for working? Where does that lead? Does your body ache and moan after a long shift? Aren't you tired waiting for people? Serving them?"

Tanya let her breath fall out of her. Her shoulders fell. She looked away out a nearby window to the business buildings of the downtown area.

"You think that you want to stay in the service industry forever?"

"We all have to serve someone, Bryan…I have to go. Be safe and please, try not to get hurt."

Tanya stood up. She walked over to Bryan's seat and he stood. They hugged. She let go of him. She squeezed his arm.

"Seriously don't get injured, okay? You'll never know when you need to use that body of yours."

"Okay, I'll see you in a few months."

Bryan walked downstairs. Sam was standing behind

the bar slowly polishing a glass. A man in a suit sat at the brass counter eating.

"So you're off?"

Sam extended his hand.

"Yeah, my flight is tonight."

Bryan shook his hand.

"All right, good luck. Kick some ass."

Sam pulled his coworker into him.

"Fuck one of them ladyboys for me. I've always wondered what it's like."

Bryan laughed and let his hand go.

He walked out to his car. A parking ticket lay under his windshield wiper. He crumbled the ticket up. It was too expensive to pay right now, he thought. He sat in the driver seat and turned on the ignition.

•••

The small restaurant was busy. Having no doors the building was open to the traffic on the country road. Motorbikes zipped by leaving trails of dust that drifted into the establishment. A lean cow bellowed in the distance, her mooing reverberating across the flat plains of Isaan, the northeastern plateau area of Thailand.

Bryan and Ploy sat across from each other. He wondered if he would kiss her that evening. It was the first date in which a companion didn't accompany her.

Ploy pushed the wicker basket of rice towards Bryan.

"You don't want to eat any more sticky rice?"

The rice sat on a small piece of plastic inside of a weaved basket. A plate of *som tum* sat next to it. The salad was a mix of raw papaya mashed with nuts, lime, fish sauce, and shrimp.

Ploy pushed her finger against her nose, making it spread out across her face slightly.

"If you eat too much it will make your nose go flat."

He nodded and scooped out a bit of the rice and dipped it in the remnants of the *som tum*. It burned his lips as he ate. She looked at him expectantly. She put her hands on the table.

Her hands were delicate. Each fingernail was painted a light pink. She tapped the edges of her nails on the table. They beat a soft staccato.

He put his hand on hers. She turned her hand over so that their palms met. He squeezed softly. He looked at her.

"What do you want to do?"

"It's so late."

He nodded. His hand rose in the air. A server nearby came over.

"Check *bin na krap.*"

The server nodded and walked away.

Bryan could feel his shoulders begin to ache. He wanted some liniment.

"Why don't we go for a little bit of a ride at least? I want to buy some *namman muay.*"

"Okay *na.*"

The bill came and Bryan paid it. The food cost ten dollars. Bryan had gotten good at currency conversion. The two rose from their seats and walked out of the establishment. The town was slow. While a short distance from Bangkok, the area still had the feel of rural living.

He'd met Ploy at a cafe. He'd gone there after training to read. She was visiting her grandmother in Isaan during a break in school. She was from Bangkok.

He'd ordered his coffee and sat down. The caffeine was a luxury. It cost him a dollar. The second time he went she approached him. The two had chatted. Ploy practiced her British accented English. He admired her forwardness. She admired his earnestness. They began to meet regularly and Bryan invited her out. She'd been accompanied by a giggling girlfriend the first two outings. It was odd. Everything moved at a slower pace out here, Bryan thought.

The two went outside and got on his motorbike, which he'd rented for the duration of his stay in the town since the area was spread out, making walking impossible. The heat of the summer didn't help. There wasn't much in the town. Bryan would ride on the dirt roads and watch the anorexic cows graze on grass as their owners watched television and drank soda.

Ploy sat on the back of his bike and hugged Bryan. The pharmacy was two kilometers from the restaurant. Despite the heat, Bryan felt a chill in the air as he drove the motorbike. Ploy scooted closer to him.

They pulled to a stop and entered the store. Owned and operated by an old man, the pharmacy also served as the man's house, with the shop taking up the front half of the building, his small living quarters visible in the back. The pharmacist looked lazily at Bryan as he walked in.

Bryan walked through the aisles. He felt out of place amongst the rows of product. He heard Ploy behind him talking to the pharmacist and then grabbing a few things. He looked at the boxing liniment on a shelf. The orange liquid was primarily menthol and its heat burned the body. He'd had the other boxers give him a rub down with the oil. It made his pores open with a scalding heat. The burning irritation made him jump up from the massage and run to the shower. The boxers wondered where he had gone. He attempted to wash off the heat and the boiling liquid to no avail. When he emerged from the shower, his skin still red and raw, the Thais looked at him, laughed, and told him to shadowbox.

He picked up the smallest bottle. It cost thirty *baht*, one dollar. He needed more but didn't want to pay. The next biggest bottle cost fifty *baht*. He calculated his costs again. The cost of training twice a day was 12,000 *baht*, four hundred dollars, for the month. The motorbike was 3,000 *baht* plus petrol. Room and board at the camp cost another four hundred dollars. Ploy stood at the counter.

Bryan walked up with the smallest bottle. He figured he could make the liquid last somehow. Everything counts in even small amounts, he thought. Ploy was waiting for him. On the counter was a bottle of shampoo, hair conditioner, and a nail file. Ploy looked at him expectantly.

"You pay okay *na*?"

She rested her hand on his arm. He felt the tips of her fingernails on his skin and the warmth of her palm. He looked at her and she met his eye.

"Okay *na*?"

He paid. They got back on the bike. He turned the ignition, the bike rumbled to a start, and they drove away.

•••

Bryan and Bee ran along the edge of the *khlong*. The long canal was filled with dirty brown water. Bryan stared into it as he ran alongside his Thai stablemate. The water remained motionless. The afternoon sun scorched the plateau drying out the walls of the *khlong*. The watermarks from the last rain were long gone, replaced by cracks created by the punching rays of the sun.

Bryan heard the whine of a motorbike. Pebbles shook underneath the motorbike's wheels, jumping to and fro as the bike passed the boxers. The muffler emitted a cough of black smoke; Bee's and Bryan's lungs reacted in kind. Bee stopped jogging. Bryan looked over his shoulder and saw Bee hacking. Bryan put his hand on Bee's back.

"Okay *mai*?"

"Okay, *mai pen rai.*"

Bee smiled, nodded and pointed forward.

The sun beat down. Bryan took the bottom of his shirt and used it to wipe his brow. Bee didn't sweat a drop. Bryans clothes were drenched. The Thai began to walk as the two neared camp.

The three trainers at the camp were lying in the ring with their arms sprawled out. Each took up a different section of ring, wanting the shade provided by the canopy over the ring to keep them cool. Tao, the head trainer, sat up when the two came in.

"You, you, quick."

The trainer made a motion as if he was wrapping his hands and laid back down enjoying the comfort of the shade for a few more minutes.

Bryan went into his room. The studio bedrooms were built to accommodate foreigners like him and were lined up in a building next to the ring. The bedroom was minimalistic with two beds, only one of which was occupied, a dresser, and a desk. A sink and mirror were at the far wall next to a rack for clothes. Attached to the main room was a small bathroom with a toilet and shower. Bryan grabbed a pair of clean wraps from the rack and exited.

He sat down on the edge of the ring and rolled his wraps into tight balls. With meticulous care he covered his knuckles and supported his wrists with the line of cloth. He stood up and began to shadowbox.

"*Reo, reo, reo.*"

A young boy sat at the edge of the ring letting his legs dangle off the side. He was the round clock for the gym, crying out the minutes that passed.

The trainers got up, stretched and put on their belly pads, shin pads, and kick pads.

Tao was in his mid-thirties and built like his name, a turtle. His body was a barrel and his head small. He nodded at Bryan. The worn gloves of the gym fit well on Bryan's hands. Tao helped him tie the strings that laced the gloves.

Bryan began his five-round training session, each round was four minutes long. A round in a fight would only be three minutes. Tao had him working on his rhythm encouraging him to move forward with style and grace instead of lumbering forward.

"*Jai yen, yen.*"

Bryan nodded and took a big breath as he stepped forward. Tao kicked him. A flash of anger passed through the foreigner's face.

"*Jai yen, yen.*"

The trainer smiled slightly and kicked Bryan's arm again. Bryan blocked with an impassive face.

The frustration was mounting in Bryan's heart. He took another breath and felt Tao kick him again. The four-minute rounds dragged on eternally. Four more rounds, three more rounds, two more rounds, Bryan thought as the pad work session came to an end.

"You, you, you stay one week more. Fight. Bee fight, you fight same day. Okay *mai?* Okay!"

The trainer pointed at the other boxer.

Bee smiled.

"Boxing, boxing."

All the motorbike drivers always catcalled Bryan as he ran along the streets, and Bee had picked up on the joke. Bee patted Bryan on the back.

"Same card, we both win *chai mai?*"

"Yeah. We will. How much do you think? If we win?"

"Oh. I don't know, bout 1500 *baht*. If gamble pay more."

Bryan began to count the cost of staying longer. He would have to use his credit card to support himself. He would have to pay to push back his flight. He would have to spend more on training, on room and board at the camp, and there was Ploy.

He stepped out of the ring and moved to a row of heavy bags and began to hit them, trying to remind himself to stay calm no matter his miscalculations.

A tractor rumbled down the road, momentarily drowning out the noise of the boxers.

♦♦♦

The van rolled through the rural landscape into the capital while Bryan attempted to sleep. His head bounced on the window, preventing him from dozing off.

The boys stumbled out of the van after the long drive to Bangkok. Bee poked Bryan in the ribs.

Bryan got out of the van slowly. His eyes squinted. The city was dull gray. The ring was surrounded by a blue tarp. The plastic cloth was ten feet high. Tao, Bee and the others walked into the fenced area. The ring sat in the middle of the grounds. A few folding chairs were splayed randomly on the cement. Streetlights lit the area.

"You, you, come here."

Tao picked up a chair from the ground and set it up. He took another and placed it backwards in front of him. He motioned for Bryan to sit down. Bryan set his wrists on the back of the chair. Tao picked up his right hand and massaged it. Bryan squeezed his hand into a fist then let go. Tao took out cloth bandages from a small bag and began to wrap Bryan's hands. Tao put his hands over Bryan's, closing the *farang's* fingers.

"*Gum mud.*"

Tao pulled Bryan's fingers open.

"*Beh.*"

Tao secured the bandage around his wrist. Over and over Tao wrapped Bryan's hands with the bandages, then lashed down the cloth with rows of medical tape. The trainer made small joints of tape and laid them across Bryan's knuckles, then put more tape over them. The foreigner had a large solid cast on his hand.

"Okay *mai*?"

Bryan clenched his fist. It felt solid. When he opened his hand it strained against the wraps, wanting to return to its fist shape.

"You, you *pai.*"

Tao pointed to mats on the ground nearby and waved Bee over. Bryan laid down on the mats and one of the gym boys began to massage boxing liniment into his skin. The orange menthol liquid burned as it set in. He breathed in and out as it scalded, knowing that in a few minutes the initial heat would loosen his muscles. He yearned for a shower, for coolness.

When the boys were done, Tao came over. He shoved a steel cup into Bryan's hands. The groin protector dangled on three strings. Tao tugged at Bryan's shorts and Bryan pulled them down. Bryan felt naked as he held the metal over his genitals. Tao stood behind him and fastened the strings tight. I'll never ask for my girlfriend to wear a thong again, Bryan thought.

Bryan squatted to make sure the cup fit snuggly. He put on his fighting shorts and began to shadowbox.

"Fight next."

The trainer took some Vaseline and smothered it on Bryan's face, wiping it along his brows, nose, and chin. He wiped a swab of the thick gel onto his chest and put gloves onto Bryan. The gloves were smelly from sweat and still wet from a previous boxer. The stuffing was worn, the strings browned with sweat. Tao tied them, securing the gloves on Bryan. Tao put a *mongkol*, a ceremonial headdress that bestowed good luck, on Bryan's head and prayed.

"Okay, *chok dee*."

Bryan walked barefoot up to the ring. He looked over his shoulder to see Bee. The younger fighter smiled at him and punched in the air.

"Fight, fight."

The whining drone of the *ram muay* music began and Bryan sealed the ring by walking along the ropes. Bee had told Bryan to do so in order to keep bad spirits from entering the ring. Bryan thought it was superstitious. He stretched against the ropes as he watched his Thai opponent do the *wai khru*. The dance paid tribute to the boxer's camp, parents, and trainer. Tao gave him a sip of water and the referee motioned for them to come together. The referee spoke quickly and checked their groins, knocking against their steel cups, then motioned them to open their mouths, checking for gum shields.

The bell rang. Bryan took it slow and easy in the first round, attempting to learn his opponent's rhythm and test him for weaknesses. He swatted at his opponent's face with a jab. Bryan received a body kick in return. His arm ached. The Thai looked calm, oblivious to the pain he'd caused. The muscles in Bryan's face relaxed, drooping down. He tried not to worry about getting hit, but the thought was fastened to him like the leather gloves on his hands. Stepping forward Bryan rotated his right hip, standing up on his left foot and letting his right leg swing like a baseball bat. Bryan hit his opponent with his shin. The Thai man, barely past the age of boyhood, was far more stoic about pain than Bryan. The Thai's face registered nothing. Taking no account of Bryan's blow the Thai kicked Bryan back, smashing his shin again into Bryan's arm. The bell rang. Bryan returned to his corner. Tao slid out a giant metal pan to catch the extra water spilled during the break. Tao put a red stool on the pan. Bryan sat and gasped for air. His lungs opened and closed holding no oxygen in. Tao spoke excitedly. Bryan tried to understand.

"*Tee Kao! Tee Kao!*"

Tao hosed him down with water and gave him some to sip. The water felt replenishing, drying up the desert of his body. The bell rang and the second round began.

The action was immediate. The Thai no longer thought of waiting, of probing for weakness, he attacked, kicking heavily. Bryan worried of the painful interest of each blow, he could only be hit so many times, each strike that landed sunk him into a deeper recession. Bryan stepped forward rising on the ball of his left foot and leaned back as his knee thrust at the Thai's stomach. He landed the knee. The Thai let out a woosh. The Thai smiled, breaking the plane of his face with a grin that showed the cheap plastic of his mouth guard. Bryan attempted to pike his opponent with his knee again when he felt the Thai's elbow cut into his forehead. The blow felt like a combination between a baseball bat and a knife, smashing and slicing. The cut hemorrhaged out red liquid, each moment that passed more blood leaked out. Bryan felt a confused concussion. The tight canvas floor wobbled and began to incline. He lurched as the ring went up. The vessel of his body staggered trying to stay upright. The ground was so near. He thrust his fist out. His cross hit his opponent. The ring leveled but still wobbled, there was still the debt in the scoring. His mind was confused. He couldn't see what was happening. The Thai came forward. He was smiling. Why was he smiling? The bell rang. The Thai shook his head. Bryan had lost the round 10-8. He would have to win the next three rounds to come ahead.

Bryan looked at his corner. The metal pan came out. The red stool sat on top of the pan. Bryan felt cold metal beneath his feet. Tao wiped blood from Bryan's face. He slathered Vaseline on Bryan's brow and screamed again and again.

"*Tee kao! Tee kao pai tii tong!*"

Tao pantomimed a knee. Bryan nodded. He wanted it to be over. He wanted to vomit. He wanted to lie down. He wanted some water. He wanted the ache to leave. He stood up. He wanted to not be confused. He wanted the fog of concussion to leave. It had cost him to come. If he won, he would earn something…money, experience, attention, the girl, something…He decided he would get his money's worth of pain, that was what it was in the ring, and that was what he earned, pain, and somehow the pain would be worth it.

The bell rang. The Thai made it to the center of the ring and waited for the *farang*. Bryan stood. He walked forward. He met the Thai in the center of the ring. The Thai kicked. Bryan stepped and stabbed the Thai with his pike-like knee in his liver. The Thai crumbled.

Bryan looked at his opponent. He wondered what he had done. The referee pointed towards a neutral corner and Bryan made his way over. The countdown began. Bryan looked into the crowd. Bee gave him a thumbs up. The referee finished the count and waved the fight off.

The Thai's corner jumped into the ring and pulled their ward out. The referee raised Bryan's hand into the air and motioned him out of the ring.

Tao took Bryan to a folding chair near the ring. Bryan sat down. A man walked over and pulled at Bryan's face. The cut bled. The man swabbed the cut with alcohol and then stitched Bryan's eyebrow with a wire-like thread.

Bryan picked up his cheap phone and dialed Ploy.

"*Hallo ka.*"

"I won, I won."

"Oh, oh, good. How much you win?"

Bryan looked around excitedly. Tao was next to the victorious Bee. He had won his fight on points, outscoring his opponent with a barrage of kicks.

"One minute."

He walked over to Tao and handed the phone to him. Tao talked quickly then handed the cellphone back to Bryan.

"Bryan."

"Yeah."

"They gave your winnings to your opponent for gas money. They said he needed it more. Fighting is his job and he lost. He needed the money. It was 800 *baht*."

"Oh."

"When you come back?"

"I don't know. I told you I leave in two days. I might go to Bangkok. It's too expensive for me to rearrange my ticket to see you again."

Silence filled the other end of the line.

"*Farang kee nok.*"

Bryan shuddered from Ploy's cheap insult.

"Ploy."

The line went dead.

He looked out into the street past the blue tarp. The street was still, packed with cars in traffic waiting for their turn to move forward.

•••

The plane ride back was long. It didn't seem that way when his journey began. He stared out the window the entire flight. The clouds didn't move. He felt as if he was forever stagnant.

The airplane landed. He felt it bump and slowly taxi to the gate. He waited patiently in his seat. He closed his eyes and wondered why he'd come back. He stood up and got his bag from the overhead compartment. The line of passengers took ten minutes to clear out. He walked down the aisle and into the airport terminal.

"Everything is English."

He walked through the airport and to the public transit system. It was slow and expensive. The sun was rising and leaked its rays into the train.

The train stopped. He walked off the train. His house was a few blocks away. The room was sublet while he was gone. The sublet had left and the room was empty save a bed, an empty dresser, and an equally empty closet. He set his bags down. The bed was bare, no sheets. He lay down.

The light poured in from the windows, his forearm blocked enough for him to sleep.

He woke up. The sun had begun to fall towards the horizon. He unpacked his bags and went into the basement and hauled up the boxes that housed his possessions. He took out clothes he hadn't worn in months. He smelled them, they didn't stink of moth balls.

The ride to the restaurant didn't take long, he took the train again.

"Bryan, how was it?"

Sam stood behind the bar.

"Good."

He beckoned Bryan to come closer. Bryan walked to the bar. Sam leaned over.

"So did you?"

"Did I what?"

"You know, ladyboys? How much did it cost?"

Bryan shook his head.

Tanya walked down the stairs. She wore a knee-length

brown skirt, flats, and a white blouse. Bryan raised his eyebrows as their eyes met.

"I'm the assistant manager. How are you doing, Bryan? Oh, you're hurt! You still have stitches. What happened? Are you going to be okay?"

"I was cut in a fight."

"Oh my. Are you okay? I was so worried for you before. Is your head okay? Are you dizzy, do you need to sit down?"

"Leave him alone. He's tough. Look at him. He came back,"

Sam walked back down the bar. He looked at Bryan over his shoulder.

"Let's get a beer soon, you can tell me all about your adventures."

"Is James here?"

"Yeah he's here. Why, are you looking to work again? You still have stitches. Should you even be working?"

"I need to work."

"Did it cost a lot to be out there? I thought it was inexpensive out there. Oh here's James."

The manager patted Bryan on the back as he walked by.

"So our hero has returned. How was it?"

"Good."

"Excellent. So how can I help you? Do you want back on the schedule?"

"Yeah that would be great."

"All right I'll throw you on. Actually, one of the new girls called in sick for tomorrow, do you want to cover her shift?"

"Sure."

"Don't you think that's a little soon? When do you get your stitches out? He still has a large cut on his face. What will the customers think?" Tanya's voice fell with her speech.

"Oh quit wringing your hands. We like our men to look like men here."

Bryan nodded.

"Okay see you tomorrow morning, I got things to do. It was great seeing you, Bryan." James patted Bryan on the back and walked away.

Bryan nodded again. Tanya reached out and squeezed Bryan's arm.

"Well, I suppose I should get to things as well. It was great talking to you. Be careful, Bryan. If you keep fighting it might really hurt you."

"There are costs to everything."

Tanya's mouth turned down.

"Well, I'll see you soon."

Bryan walked out of the restaurant. He walked to the train station. The train slid up before him. Its doors opened. He wondered when he would be out of debt. He wondered when the costs would disappear. He let his fingers touch the hard threads of his stitches. The doors of the train closed.

The Boxer's Soliloquy

The world was dark, and now…it wobbles. How much of my life have I missed? The count is, is four, four already. Stay down; get up? Stay down; get up? My head hurts, the world spins. Stay down; get up?

I would see her, sitting by the pool. She is gone, sitting there no longer, nor here, by the ring.

It was back and forth, body punches, clinched up, umph, esh, umph, uppercut, spin out, jab, jab. Where was it, the one that I didn't see? Breathe in, breathe out. The world—is it staying still for me?

How many seconds have passed? Can I stand? Should I take more time on my knees? Breathe in, breath in, breathe out. The referee keeps counting. This should end. He counts so fast.

The world teeters under my feet. It sways. He wipes my gloves. The other man with gloves is coming. Cover. Spin out. Umph, jab, jab, cross…The gloves are so thin. Can he feel my punches? Can he feel pain? Cross, hook, he should have felt that one…His expression is empty. Everything is so slow.

There is that voice. That voice. From my corner, telling me...something—I can't hear, there is only the sound of sweat and leather.

The pool outside the house smelled like chlorine. She was tanning herself in the sun. Reading; she was always reading. Taking her time. I think her books were her escape, then she escaped. It gave me more time to focus, to focus.

Umph, block, cover, body, head, body, body...When will it end? I don't know where the clock is. Will the referee count the passing time for me?

A Fighter's Heart

He shifted around on the bed. She put her arm on his chest. She stroked him slowly.

"I like that you're in shape…you're so dedicated and manly."

Her voice had been a schoolgirl's. She laughed lightly. She put her head on his left pectoral and listened to his heartbeat. He slowed his breath down. He closed his eyes. She was warm against him. He hadn't seen her in a week. He was working nights at the restaurant and training early in the morning. He imagined himself moving about the ring, throwing punches, slamming elbows, smashing his shins, and piercing his knees into a faceless opponent. He slowed his breathing even more. He looked at her. She had clear green eyes, they reminded him of spring leaves, light green and almost translucent. He saw his reflection in her eyes. He kissed her. She climbed on top of him. She leaned over and kissed him more.

"Let's have sex."

"I can't."

"You read that article, too, there is no reason not to. You're not fighting for a week."

She moved her hand from his chest to his lower abdomen.

"I'm tired."

He looked away. He could feel his erection growing. "Tired?"

"I have to get up early. I need to go to sleep."

She sighed and rolled off of him. The fights were more often and the pattern had picked up in pace. He would fight. She would lie in bed waiting for him. He would come home exhausted. He would want rest. She would want something more. She would stay awake while he slept.

She waited for his breathing to slow to a state of slumber then rose from the bed. She moved into her small kitchen with her copy of *Norweigan Wood* in hand and began to read it.

•••

Bryan and Sam stood by the bar. A couple of girls came up looking to order a drink. Sam turned to them.

"This is Bryan. He's a fighter. He can fucking kick some ass."

The girls nodded. Sam nodded with them.

"He actually fought yesterday, he won of course."

One of the girls looked at Bryan. The other looked at Sam. Both had matching looks of indifference. One of the girls tried to move past Sam.

"Cool."

"He fought this shorter guy. The shorter guy was really

fucking tough. He kept kicking Bryan in the legs. Kapow!"

Sam swung his arms across his chest, making the motion of a leg kick.

"Every time the short guy would throw a bunch of punches then bang, Bryan would get kicked! Right in the leg but Bryan is no fucking chump. He grabbed the shorter guy and fucking kneed him in the gut. And then he elbowed him in the head. The short guy was real fucked up by the fourth round. He had blood streaming down his face. The doctor looked at his cuts and called the fight. It was awesome."

"Sounds like it."

The other girl turned away from the men.

"Let's go get drinks at the other bar."

She clasped her hand in her friend's hand and they walked off, leaving Sam and Bryan on the bar patio.

Sam and Bryan had gotten cut from the restaurant early. The downtown business was going through a slow period. All their coworkers talked about how things were slowing down, how the recession was impacting sales. The slump in the economy didn't seem to affect Sam; he simply drank it away.

"What's fighting like?"

Sam's trim beard aged his youthful face with a light carpet of maturity. He looked at Bryan with blue eyes that peered out of his sloped forehead. The blue of Sam's eyes were like fragments of a summer sky.

"It's like swimming in a sea of gelatin, a thick soup. I don't know. It's like being smacked around in the ocean by a monster that is both the other person and yourself."

He dropped his gaze to his beer. It was his third. No point in stopping now, he thought to himself. He felt a buzzing in his pocket. He took out his cell phone and looked at the text message. She'd written him.

"Busy, can we get together later this week…? I know we had plans."

Sam put his hand on Bryan's shoulder. Bryan looked up from his phone. Sam finished his beer with a long gulp.

"That's so awesome. I gotta say, I really respect you man. You're doing it, wait right here."

Sam went off in the direction of the bar. After a few moments he came back with two shots. He gave one to Bryan.

"Cheers to victory."

He clinked his dose of well liquor on Bryan's.

"To victory."

•••

Bryan first met her at the park. He'd been reading his second Murakami novel. She slowed her jogging to a halt in front of him.

"I started running because of that book."

Bryan looked up at her. The sun lit her face. She waited a moment.

"Did you know Murakami is an avid runner? He start-ed at the age of thirty-three. He does a marathon every year. He's been doing one every year for the past twenty years."

She looked at him expectedly. He looked down at the book. He looked up at her. The sun was behind her so it was hard for him to make her out. He'd seen her jog around the lake every day for two months. He liked to come out and sit on the bench after he had his breakfast, before work, or before going to the gym to train. He'd read for twenty minutes to start his day, weather permitting.

"Did you like the book?"

He moved over on the bench, hoping that she'd join him. She looked at the empty space on the bench. Bryan looked at the spot and then looked at her.

"I did."

She pursed her lips and touched her hair.

"It's a beautiful love story, it's so ordinary, and yet so realistic. Murakami really has a way of writing."

"I'm not that far into it. The lead character, Toru, has just moved into his college dorm."

"Can I see the book?"

She took the novel and began to read. He watched her green eyes scan the pages. She sat down next to him. Her brown hair was held back with a hairband. She wore running shoes, shorts, and an athletic top. The morning sun lit the pages of the book.

"I like reading a little bit of books that I've read before. If I read just a page or two the whole story comes back to me. I like that rush of memory. It's like a waterfall of images, and then sometimes I remember where I was and what I was doing when I read the book."

"I've always wanted to read a good love story. One of the other waiters where I work suggested it."

"Well, they were right. It is a good love story, although I hate how Toru seems to let life happen to him. You'll see what I mean later on in the book."

"Yeah, I guess, so. I'll keep what you said in mind."

His eyes caught hers. He let himself fall into the light green of her irises then he let his gaze slide off of her. He cleared his throat.

"So I see you running here every day. What do you do when you're not running?"

"I'm in college, a women's studies major. And what about you, what do you do when you're not reading?"

"I'm a boxer, Muay Thai."

•••

The restaurant was winding down for the evening when Tanya walked up to him.

"Bryan, can we talk?"

He was rolling silverware, one of his closing duties.

"Sure."

Bryan got up from his seat and followed Tanya to the office.

"Take a seat."

Tanya motioned to the cheap chair on the other side of the office desk. Tanya sat in her office chair. Her short frame was raised by its height.

"You're a good worker. And obviously your coworkers like you a lot."

Bryan looked at the desk. It had a few papers on it, a calendar, a computer, a stack of eggshell white business cards with Tanya's name and title: assistant manager. Her long black hair hung low and her dark eyes searched Bryan's face, looking for the right words. Her pupils focused, becoming darker

"You can't come in all banged up. I know you just had a fight but you need to be able to walk and you can't come in with black eyes. We rely on a regular clientele. Having your face battered and bruised is threatening to them."

Bryan nodded. Tanya sighed and clicked her finger-nails on the desk.

"I always thought it was okay. I've been getting my shifts covered if I haven't been able to work."

Tanya pursed her glossy lips at Bryan.

"Originally I thought it was okay…but now. How long Bryan? I think you should really reconsider what you're doing. You're smart, why don't you go back to college?"

"Back to college?"

•••

Bryan's cell phone vibrated in his pocket. He pulled it out and read the text from her.

"Want to get together today?"

Bryan held the cell phone loosely in his hand then began to text back.

"Yeah I'd like that."

A message came up a few moments later.

"What do you want to do?"

"Let's go to the park. I'll meet you there."

Bryan was early. He sat on the bench and watched the lake before him. The lake was over three miles long. Joggers passed by him, their shoes pitter-pattered on the cement path. He picked up a stone and threw it into the water. The stone skipped twice. He watched the ripples fade.

"Hey."

She stood a foot or two away from him.

"Hey."

He walked towards her and took her hand. She flinched away from him. Her green eyes looked dark. She looked back at him.

"We need to talk."

He turned to face the water. She looked at his profile. They stood in silence. She stuck her hands into her pockets.

"I'm not getting what I'm needing. Your elaborate ritual of touching other men is getting in the way of our relationship."

She felt the piece of paper in her pocket; she wrapped it around her hand.

"Your constant emphasis on discipline is constraining our desires, we don't even touch each other anymore."

He turned and faced her. Her body tensed. He took a breath in and then let out a slow exhale.

"You sound like one of your essays."

"How long have we been together?"

Bryan began to mark the months off by the amounts of fights he'd had. Ploy had never asked these questions, but this girl wasn't Ploy.

"I thought I was straightforward with you about what I do."

"I'm unhappy."

She began to sob. Small trickles of tears ran down her face. Her shoulders shuddered.

"I'm not happy."

He took a step forward, and she walked into his arms. Her body vibrated against his as she cried. He held her.

"I'm so confused…" Her words were choked by tears.

She stroked his muscular arms as he held her. She felt safe against the world but felt wary of him.

"It's okay."

He looked into the water. She'd told him his eyes were so light they seemed translucent. She could only see her own light reflection in them. They were devoid of color. He wondered what color they were now.

"Let's go home, I'll read to you. Tomorrow morning we'll go running together."

A Puncher's Chance

The room phone rang. It rang again. Sam opened his eyes. His mouth tasted like shit. His eyes focused angrily on the phone. He leaned over and picked up the receiver.

"Mister Brown, this is your eleven a.m. wake-up call. You are scheduled for a late check out at two o'clock."

Sam set down the receiver. He was still wearing his full set of clothes, wrinkled from sleep. He checked his messages on his phone; an insistent message from Tanya at work, and another from an unknown number. His shoes were still on. He put his hands in his pocket and felt the crumpled ticket.

•••

"That was a hell of a fight."

The man slapped Bryan on the back.

"Can I buy you a beer?"

"I got one."

Bryan pulled the bottle up from between his legs. The alcohol had been icing the inside of his thigh, which was mottled yellow and purple. The liquid was now warm.

Bryan took the check out of his wallet. He looked at it again. The two thousand dollars had already been spent; the actual money was just waiting to be circulated. Money isn't owned, he thought, it is spent.

He crumpled the check in his hand.

●●●

Sam's hands shook. He picked his cards back up again, pocket kings. He had made a set on the flop and pushed all in. He set his hand back down.

The sound of chips stacking, falling, and shuffling filled the Vegas poker room. An empty beer bottle sat in a holder next to Sam. He flagged down the cocktail waitress.

"Another beer and a shot of Jameson."

The waitress nodded. He watched her walk away.

He looked back at the game.

"Texas hold'em, the Cadillac of poker. Who's ready to lose their paycheck?"

The other players were placid in their seats. They'd heard it all before. The dealer pointed his hand at one of the players.

"Call, raise, or fold."

The middle-aged man looked at his cards again, and looked at the board.

"Call."

The other two players on the man's left folded.

The dealer dealt out the last two cards.

"Show 'em."

Sam put down his cards face up.

"Three kings."

He waited expectantly for the pile to be pushed to him.

"Eight, and nine...of hearts."

Sam looked down at the board, seeing the other three hearts. He groaned.

"Flush."

The dealer pushed the stack of chips towards the winner. Sam pushed away from the table. His eyes focused on his ruined cards.

"Some guys have all the luck, all the fucking luck."

Sam's face flushed red with anger. He should have won.

"What's the minimum buy in?"

"One hundred dollars."

Sam opened his wallet and ruffled through the bills, counting only fifty dollars total.

"Save my seat."

He got up and walked to the ATM. He withdrew three hundred dollars on a cash advance from his credit card. When he returned to his seat the waitress came by with his beer and shot.

"Another round."

He downed the shot and half the beer a moment after she set down the drinks.

Sam's hands weren't shaking anymore. His face was red with the heat of alcohol. He'd get his money back, he thought.

He bought back in for one hundred and fifty dollars. The dealer pushed the chips at him. He shuffled them; the sound of the pieces soothed him. It was the sound of a future about to be fulfilled.

•••

Bryan wanted the fight to be over. He was sick of waiting. He was tired of sitting. He was hungry. The weight-cutting was long over but he still felt empty.

The commission was watching over the amateur fighters getting their hands wrapped. Bee was laying on the floor nearby.

"Bryan, why they look?"

"*Kwam bpen farang*, they are foreigners."

Bee shrugged and looked back down.

Bryan had helped the fighter get on the card. He'd helped Bee get his visa to come over so that he could fight in the States. Thai fighters were a draw because of their ethnicity and style, almost the same as *farang* back in Thailand, Bryan thought. Bee looked at him, then laughed.

"Wut the fuk?"

Bryan had managed to get on the same card. His last fight had been in Thailand. When he came home he needed the fight for the money. He didn't want to go back to working at the restaurant again.

•••

Sam got up from the poker table. He looked at his watch. He still had plenty of time, he thought.

He looked down. The carpeting was all the same. The lights were all set to a perpetual twilight. He eventually found his way out of the labyrinth. The bright desert sun hit his eyes and he winced with shock. Beads of perspiration began to roll down his forehead. He squinted as a drop of sweat fell into his eye.

He walked up the strip. The casinos were elaborate palaces set beside the road. The entrances to them were accessible and at the same time foreign.

Sam's shirt was wet. It clung to him. He wanted a drink. The alcohol was seeping out of his pores.

A row of Latino men stood on the sidewalk. They wore baseball caps. They didn't sweat. The men clicked and flicked a handful of cards in their hands. It sounded like a horde of crickets. As he walked by the men the last one handed him a card. It was for a strip club.

Sam wanted to see it. He wanted it more than anything else. He didn't know where the club was but was sure he could get there. He walked.

The heat made him feel dizzy. He stopped at a gift shop at the north end of the strip. They sold T-shirts, magnets, and beer. He bought the latter and a pack of gum.

"Do you know where I could print something out?"

The cashier pointed across the street.

He downed the beer and then began chewing on the gum. His mouth tasted like mint flavored malt liquor.

"Do you have computers?"

The woman at the copy shop pointed. He thought about how she would never make it as a stripper. He printed out his resume. He bought a folder.

The cold and then the heat will give me the sickness, he thought as he stepped back into the desert sun. He walked west.

He saw a strip club. He was thirsty. Next to the club was a bar. He walked in.

"I just moved into town. I'm living right off the strip."

He thought himself a great liar.

The bartender nodded and held out his hand.

Sam gave him his resume.

"You want something?"

"Not yet, not yet."

Sam walked out.

•••

"Sit, sit, no sit."

Bryan sat on the ground.

"No sit. Sit."

Bee placed his hand flat on the ground.

Bryan lay down.

The floor was carpeted like every other part of the casino. The pattern played itself over and over all over the casino floor. Bryan put his face against it.

Bee opened a bottle of boxing liniment.

"Off."

Bee pulled Bryan's shirt over his arms.

Bee dumped the orange liquid on Bryan's back and began to lightly massage his back.

An official came over.

"What are you doing?"

"Massage, massage, you want massage… misstaaah-hh?"

Bee giggled.

"You can't use that oil back here. Weren't your bags checked? That's not part of the rules. Stop now or I'll have to disqualify you both."

Bee looked confused.

"*Arai wa*!? Wat da fuk?"

Bryan sat up. He looked at the official.

"Sorry we didn't realize the ointment wasn't allowed."

He looked at Bee and shook his head. Bee shrugged and put the cap on the ointment. He sat down and put on his headphones. The sound of Carabao emitted from them.

•••

The hostess looked up at him from behind thick glasses. Her dark hair had blonde streaks in it. She was reading a book. Her breasts were pinched together by a push-up bra. Sam ogled her.

"Fifteen dollars."

She tapped her nails against the stand.

Sam opened his wallet.

"Do you have an ATM?"

She pointed to one just by the entry.

He pulled out his credit card and withdrew $200. He gave her a crisp twenty.

The strip club was loud. The noise filled the room. The plush seats were empty. A girl stood lackluster by the pole. Her eyes followed Sam when he came in.

He went to the bar. A few girls were sitting on couches.

His cellphone buzzed. He looked at it. It was the restaurant. He let it go to voicemail.

A new song came on. The stripper walked to the pole and wiped it down with a spray bottle and some paper towels. She put her tools aside and swiveled around the pole.

Sam followed her with his eyes.

She climbed up the pole and slid down. She tossed off her top and pushed her breasts against the floor-to-ceiling rod.

Sam felt flushed.

When the song was over she walked to Sam.

•••

Bryan felt jittery. His skin prickled, it was a mass of goosebumps in the desert heat. He looked down at his hands. Bee had wrapped them. The athletic commission official kept his gaze on the Thai for the entirety of the process. Bee had had to redo them.

"Why can not do this?" Bee made a rolling movement with his hands.

Bryan shrugged.

"*Kwaam bpen farang.*"

The official reason was one of fairness and law, yet it was easiest to describe as foreign. There is no fairness, and the law can be bent, Bryan thought. The only difference between here and Thailand is that the law here is shellacked with more ornaments of process; it's no more fair. Bryan wondered how he could say that to Bee.

Bryan began to stretch, waiting for his bout.

•••

The light hit Sam's face. He walked forward. He felt for his wallet. It hardly seemed there. The fight was in an hour. He stumbled down the strip to the casino. The entrance was easy.

"Can I use my, my, card for bets?"

The cashier nodded.

He put a hundred on Bryan, and a hundred on Bee. If he won he could just deposit the money straightaway and not have to pay the overdraft fees from his credit card. He looked at his ticket. Bryan was sure to win. Sam could feel it. He walked into the venue with a sway.

A large ring sat in the middle of the small conference room. He took his seat. Bryan had gotten him a free ringside ticket. He opened his wallet. He fished out his last twenty and ordered a beer.

His cell phone buzzed. He picked it out of his pocket and read what was on the screen.

"Where are you? This is the last time, you were supposed to be here a half hour ago!"

Sam loved getting hot text messages from Tanya.

The beer felt cold in his mouth. His memory was lost for the rest of the evening.

•••

Bee fought and won. He hurriedly unwrapped and put on sweat pants. He put Bryan's *mongkol* on his head and led him to the ring. The tail threads of the *mongkol* brushed the fighter's neck as he walked forward. Bryan looked out into the crowd. Sam was sitting there. He looked drunk. Bee held down the ropes. Bryan stepped over them.

"I want a good clean fight. Obey my commands at all times. Touch gloves and when the bell rings come out fighting."

Bryan walked back to his corner. He pulled up his shorts. The Vaseline on his face felt thick. His hands bent into a permanent fist within the gloves. His belly expanded with air.

He stretched on the rope for the last few seconds bending backwards on them.

The bell rang. He walked forward into the present.

The water felt cold in his mouth. He didn't remember the round. He wouldn't remember the others.

•••

Sam stumbled out of the venue. He wanted a beer. Bryan would be out soon. He would wait for him by the bar. His phone buzzed again. It was a Vegas number. The call went to voicemail. He listened to it.

"Our bartender walked out last night, guess she can dance better than make drinks. You want a job, come in tomorrow at seven p.m."

He decided to stay in Vegas. It was a lucky town after all.

•••

"Some people, they got it. Sometimes it don't matter what's going on in the ring, a flash, then it's all over."

The official was standing over Bee as he cut the tape off Bryan's hands. He looked down and away.

Bryan nodded and looked down as well. He felt sore, and tired, and thirsty, and hungry. The official focused back on Bryan.

"Some guys have all the luck. That was real amazing. I never thought, who would have guessed, but I suppose everyone has a puncher's chance."

Immigration Song

She woke up with a sigh. Her breath fell out of her. Ploy looked over at him. His eyes were red-rimmed like hers, his from drink, hers from silent sobbing.

She got up. He didn't move. She gathered her things and went to the shower. The water was either too hot or too cold. The landlord didn't fix the shower. She learned a new vocabulary word: slumlord.

Ploy dressed. Her brown eyes scanned him. His skin was as white as a ghost's, hers was brown; he said it was tan, her friends said it was black.

He snored and smelled like a bar. The rumble of his sleep filled her ears. She wondered why she was here. She left the house for work, passing by the flowers he left her on the way out.

They'd saved up money for a car. She was happy about that. It wasn't as good as the car she had at home in Thailand, but at least she didn't have to take the bus. The early morning bus rides to the restaurant were the worst. Every single time there was the old Laos woman, crazed by loneliness, age, drink, or some other malady. As the bus swayed the woman would speak in Lao, a language close enough to Thai that she could understand the woman's sad narrative. The Lao woman would look around.

"A little leftover *som tum, lap pla duk* with rice."

The Lao woman's voice would become singsong.

"Good, Good. This year it will rain.

"Good. Good. This year the harvest.

"Good. Good. This year more *som tum, lap pla duk*. More than just rice.

"Good. Good. This year, this year…"

The old lady would pull out a photo album and slowly flip through the photographs. Each picture was of the same three people. The first set was of a parade. The figures were ornately dressed in gilded costumes. The next set they were all standing in a rice field. The sky was bright behind them. The last set had the three standing next to a *kwailek*. The iron tractor stood motionless, replacing buffaloes that had plowed the fields for decades.

As the bus stopped the Laos woman would always stare at her in with a glare of familiarity. Ploy would quickly get off the bus and walk the two blocks to the Thai restaurant she worked at.

•••

The car stopped in front of the Thai restaurant, Plearn. She got out and entered work. She opened the restaurant, setting up the tables, putting out silverware and glasses, wiping down the seats. Her coworker Pear came in. Pear always told her how lucky she was to have an American boyfriend, how Ploy would get a green card soon, how she could get a better job and not have to work hard like a rice farmer from Isaan.

They stood around for a half hour before some college students came in for lunch. The students shared a dish of pad thai and left a dollar tip.

Tae came out of the kitchen. He sat down and began to play with his phone. He'd been cooking at the restaurant for six months and was the de facto manager, as his parents owned the establishment. He disliked being in charge. When he got lonely he would sit in the dining room to be around others. He complained loudly about the customers and how his hands always smelled of fish sauce.

A few more groups of customers came in.

Ploy waited on a table of Europeans.

They paid her. She looked at the bill. The tip was only a few coins.

"Excuse me, was there something wrong with the service?"

"No."

One of the men left a few more coins on the table.

•••

She counted her money. Tae gave her thirty dollars in cash as her day's wages. Then there were her tips. She'd spent twelve hours at the restaurant, a lunch and dinner shift. She made eighty-seven dollars in tips. She sighed, glad that Bryan had bought groceries recently. Rent was due.

Ploy had never had to worry about money in Bangkok. She'd only bothered Bryan about it when they met because her grandmother told her she needed a man that would support her and that all foreigners were rich. She scared Bryan off the first time. He came back. They worked things out. She'd been happy when they were in Thailand together. And then she came here, with him.

She walked to the car. It started easily. Katy Perry was singing "California Girls" on the radio. When she lived in Bangkok she would go out to the bars in the RCA, a club district in the city, and Katy Perry would always be crooning. When she told her friends that she was moving to America they all asked for the singer's autograph. She hadn't been anywhere near Katy Perry's Hollywood.

She pulled out and began the drive home. It was dark out. Her headlights were on. The speedometer inched forward. The fuel gauge slowly declined. The thermostat began to rise. She heard a snake hiss. Steam started to emit from the engine. She pulled over. She got out her phone.

"Bryan, Bryan…Bryan."

"What's up?"

"The car. There is something the matter with it."

"What's going on? Take it easy."

"It started to steam and…"

The sound of passing cars filled her ears. Headlights flashed on her body and then disappeared in the distance.

"What should I do?"

"Can you drive?"

"The car is broke."

"So it's steaming?"

"I don't know. I don't know what's wrong."

"Where are you?"

"I pulled over."

"Okay. I'll be there as soon as I can. I just finished my cash-out at work."

•••

The cars continued to pass. She looked at her phone. If she were in Thailand she would be asleep. Her mother would be waking up and would start cleaning while the morning soap operas were on. Ploy would leave the house and go to her office job in Bangkok. The traffic would be annoying, but the car would work. She'd have meetings in air-conditioned rooms, would have lunch with her colleagues, and dinner with a group of college friends.

She wasn't in Thailand anymore.

Bryan came. He called a tow truck.

The car was pulled up onto the back of the truck. The tow truck driver had a potbelly. His breath came out in snorts. He looked piggish. His nickname would have been Oot in Thailand.

Bryan said nothing on the way home. She didn't know if he was mad. He took her hand. She tried to listen to the radio. It was country music, there was a song about a man and a woman and a highway that didn't care.

The tow truck stopped in front of a closed auto body shop. Bryan pushed the small car into a parking spot while she steered. Bryan was glad for all the squats he had done, it made the onerous task a little easier.

"I'll come back in the morning to talk to the mechanic. Let's take the bus home."

They waited at the bus stop; it took twenty minutes for a bus to arrive. She felt tired. The doors of the bus whooshed open.

The Laos woman was in the back of the bus.

"Tommorrow, tomorrow."

The Laos woman began to tap her feet as she talked.

"It will rain. Pit, pit. Good, good. Pitter patter. Good, good."

Ploy held onto Bryan's arm. The bus stopped. They got out and walked to their apartment. Once inside, she ran to the bedroom.

"*Hallo Meh? Hallo? Meh yuu nai nia*?" Her words were emptied into her mother's voicemail.

She heard Bryan sigh in the living room.

"Ploy?"

"Yes?"

"Wanna watch a movie?"

"What do you wanna watch?"

"You ever hear of The Maltese Falcon? Dashiell Hammett wrote it."

"Dashiell? I'm tired and will fall sleep."

"You fall asleep even when you're not tired."

She set down the phone. She could still hear the dial tone. Where was her mother? Everyone was gone, she didn't know where to.

Bryan was sitting on the couch. He'd showered and smelled of soap. She sat next to him.

She heard him breathe. It was a whisper. He turned his face towards hers.

"It's going to be okay. You know that right?

She leaned onto his chest and heard the song of his heart.

"I know, I know."

Stars

They weren't stars, they were discolorations, and they moved. The spots Bryan saw were blue or light red. Yes they sparkled, yes they appeared and disappeared, but no they weren't stars. Bryan didn't feel like he was seeing the heavens. He recognized the canvas underneath him and the lights illuminating the ring overhead. The stars weren't stable bits of light in the night; they shook and spun, like his legs. He wobbled like a drunk on a party boat. The referee counted. Bryan nodded. He breathed in and out. He could hear the crowd roar, it was insulting. The referee waved the fight off.

Bee took him by his arm. It was sharp and pinching. Bryan wanted the dignity to walk by himself; he wanted to recover what had slipped away minutes ago. The doctor questioned him, and he answered.

Bee sat him down and began to push out the lump under his eye with cold metal. The chill of it burned. The freezing feeling passed from under Bryan's eye to the ridge of his cheek. The metal was hard, unrelenting, and pushed the pain around. He wanted to sink his head but Bee held it up to the light.

"Look, look at me."

"I think it will be okay."

"Follow finger my."

"Maybe a little punch drunk."

"Punch drunk a little."

"Big heart?"

"Big heart always. Drink water, rest. *Sabaii*."

Bee got up. He left the back room and went to watch the rest of the fights. Bryan sat in the chair. He didn't want to get up, didn't want to see anyone. He looked up. The overhead lights were bright in his eyes. He squinted. The lights flickered as he blinked.

He went out into the convention center hall. He walked away from the fights. He found a door leading outside. The wind chilled him, raising goose bumps on his arms. He shivered. He looked up.

The night stars were static.

•••

Ploy came into the bedroom. She sat on the bed and stared at him. Her hair fell over her shoulders. It was dark like a moonless night. Her eyes were a mahogany teak. She put her hand on his arm. He winced; the bruises were deep.

Bryan hugged her. He pushed her back. She rested on her back. His reflection looked small in her eyes.

"Go ahead."

"What?"

"I know what you are going to say."

"I wasn't going to say anything."

"You think it's a bad idea."

"Yes."

"You think its bad for my body."

"What about the future? We almost have the gym and what about a family?"

"So I'll stop."

"When?"

"Now."

"Really?"

"No."

"It makes you happy."

"It does."

"It's hurting me, seeing you like this. It's so much on me."

"I know."

"I don't wanna talk about this anymore."

"I won't bring it up anymore."

"Then what else is there to talk about?"

"When will you fight next?"

•••

A cold breeze sat on his skin and fell into his bones. The bouts were outside of a casino. The sun was negotiating its way into the horizon. The moon was haggling with the sky. Glimmers of evening stars were barely visible.

The announcer called out his name. Bee held down the ropes. He stepped over them. He could hear the jeering cries of the crowd, it was insulting. His opponent stood across from him. The referee brought them together. Bryan breathed in, and then out.

The referee spoke. The fight began. Time slowed. Bells rang. People cried. Bryan hit his opponent. Bryan was hit.

Bryan hit back. He hit him again and again. His opponent fell. The referee counted. He walked to a neutral corner. And then it ended.

The referee was shouting at his opponent's corner to stay out of the ring. The trainer had a look of anguish. The fighter came to. Bryan went over to him.

"Thank you."

The fighter showed no sign of appreciation.

The announcer grabbed his hand.

"The winner by way of knock out…"

A horde of people swarmed into the ring like ants onto a sugar cube. They pointed their cameras at him. He felt Bee by his side. He knew Ploy was watching. He looked out into the seats.

The flashes shone white in his eyes. When he closed his eyes he saw faint spots of red and blue. The canvas beneath him was an anchor. He looked above the sea of flashes and into the night to see the stars. They inched across the sky.

Measured

Simon waited for a left jab from the southpaw. The jab came from the middle of the chest and stuck at him with a lazy pawing motion. Simon smacked down the gloved fist and came over the top with a left hook. The other boxer looked slightly dazed. Simon stood for a few more seconds, gauging the distance between himself and the boxer's right hand. The boxer's right hand came back, and then slowly lurched forward. Simon parried and threw a right overhand. The other boxer had his back to the corner and an open ring to his left. His left hand could almost brush the rope of the ring. The bell rang.

"You have to cut da ring. Cut da ring."

The tone of Bee's voice dipped and rose with each syllable. The voice was effeminate, but annoyance rung out. Bee would get excited during sparring yet during fights he was cool and collected. Simon was not fighting, he was sparring, so Bee yelled.

"You have to check, too. Check where he is. Punch to da body, uppercut then to head."

The bell rang again and he began to stalk the other boxer, who responded with the same lackadaisical combination. Simon continued the conversation of their bodies with left uppercuts that came in under the elbow to hit the soft side of the belly. The other boxer let out a wheeze of air and brought his fists back up. Simon pivoted on his left foot and his left fist slingshot into the other boxer's head. The other boxer looked disoriented, his eyes blinked slowly.

Bryan stood next to the seated Thai coach. Bryan had brought him on a year ago. They'd fought on the same cards together, and now they taught together. Bee dealt with the day to day training of the fighters, Bryan the gym operations.

"Go, go, go."

The bell chimed, Bryan looked at the boxers.

"Use your straight punches, long punches, Simon."

Simon took mental note and judged the distance. He threw a jab to the other boxer's head, which made the boxer's neck snap back at the same time as Simon's hand return to his guard. Simon followed his jab with a cross. The other boxer began to turn away from him. Simon moved to face him and threw a short uppercut into the other boxer's nose. Simon took a step back and waited for a moment.

The bell issued a warning. Bryan stood up from his small ringside stool.

"Go, go! You have thirty seconds."

Simon threw a cross into the boxer's skull. The punch was short and lacked the full leverage of his body. The bell rang.

"Go hit the bag, Simon."

Simon took off his headgear and sixteen-ounce gloves. He replaced his hand protection with smaller gloves. Simon began to work the heavy bag, practicing rudimentary combinations. Simon's lean, light-brown body moved as he went through the basic attacks.

He spent another hour at the gym and then got on his bicycle to ride home. He roomed in a house with two other men. Both, like Simon, were absent from the house for the majority of the day. Simon rode slowly through the downtown area, where the gym was located, into the outer edges of the projects. The house was three and a half miles from the gym, five from downtown, and four and a half from Simon's workplace. The house bordered the projects, although new condos were being built not far from his apartment.

He initially moved into the house due to the low rent but as more young people moved into the area the rent had steadily increased. When he arrived home he looked at a map of the city that hung in his room. He let his eyes wander over the nearby blocks. He traced the city streets with his fingers.

•••

Simon woke up at five thirty a.m. He went for a jog north from his house. The northern area was bombed out by the housing crisis. Many of the homes had been foreclosed. Banks gave out loans that had extended credit too far. When the financial crisis hit many lost their homes. The houses stood abandoned, the windows broken, the doors busted, the innards ravaged by locals who stripped out useful materials such as copper piping.

Simon jogged on the broken sidewalk and carved a convoluted path through the houses. He maintained a regular route. He noticed the changes in the area. This house was stripped the night before, that house had just been foreclosed, another house had just been squatted. He jogged through the area because of its uneven turf. The rest of the city was paved regularly, and running constantly on a flat, hard surface would grind at his knee joints. The upheaval of the sidewalk provided irregular pressure to his knees that would keep them strong and healthy.

As the sun rose on the project the scant rays met no one but Simon. Most of the residents wouldn't wake for several hours. Simon would be long gone from the area by the time the locals had begun their daily routine of loitering. The sun's shine barely lit Simon's path. He crunched on broken malt liquor bottles as he continued his jog. Simon ran his three-mile course and returned home. He ate some oatmeal. He looked at his cell phone. He had recently gotten it. No one had called. He biked to work.

•••

"I'm gonna pound your skull flat."

Joe was a few inches taller than Simon and had fewer tattoos, although the ones Joe had were embarrassing except to the man who wore them. On the left bicep Joe had a portrait of Bugs Bunny with an erection. The bunny's phallus was pictured holding up a dumbbell. When Bryan was especially mad at Joe he would slap the tattoo and then Joe would swear he was going to get it covered with a tribal barbed wire. Simon had a lone tattoo on his bicep of a dog, a date, and the name "Abby" in Old English. Joe danced around the ring shadowboxing.

"You ready for this? Are you ready for this?"

Simon stood in the ring. Bryan watched the boxers.

"Listen, Simon, I want you to use your uppercut. Mix up your jab with that short uppercut to the nose. Measure the distance between you two with your hands. After you throw your hand combinations, end everything with a leg kick."

Simon was preparing for a bout against a taller opponent.

"The point is to drive in and chop at the leg, chop it down like it's a tree."

•••

"Why you gotta hurt me like that, honey? I thought you were my friend."

Simon shrugged his shoulders and pointed at Bryan.

"He told me to do it."

Joe sighed.

"Well I hope he doesn't tell you to move your feet because that would make me gay."

Joe winked then sat on Simon's feet while Simon finished his sit-ups. Every day after sparring the fighters would do sit-ups together. They would weigh each other down by sitting on each other's feet.

Joe looked at Simon.

"Thirty-one, thirty-two, thirty-three, thirty-four… what are you doing tonight?"

"I might read."

"Read? Why don't you call that girl up?"

The two switched places. Simon sat on Joe's legs and began to count.

"If you fuck her we can compare notes."

"Shut up."

"Are you lovebirds done chit-chatting? Make sure you fill out your log."

Bryan sat at the gym's front desk looking at paperwork.

Joe changed and left the gym after filling out the log. The daily log was to keep track of each fighter's weight, sparring rounds, hours of training, and any small notes that they might have. Simon lingered after he showered. He slowly filled out his log and then looked up at Bryan.

"Why'd you have me spar with that guy yesterday? I felt sorry for him. He had no sense of space, all of his shots were off."

"He told me that he had a fight. He'd been talking to some promoter of his own accord. He hadn't been sparring or training but got it into his head that he was going to fight. I didn't want to rupture his dream, but did want to make him more grounded. I'm not sending guys from my gym into fights that they can't handle. Besides, he said he had one good punch, it was his 'chi punch.'"

"He loaded that punch like it was a musket."

"What's important is that you learn about distance, between yourself and the other man. You have to know how far away you are from each other, and how close. Make sure to think about your fight before you go to bed. Spend a few minutes imagining yourself in the ring with your opponent. Remember to think about that leg kick. Chop the leg."

"Thanks, Bryan."

Simon got on his bicycle to ride home. He had stopped taking the bus when he had started sparring. Although he ran daily he was still becoming fatigued while training. Bryan pointed to the corrosive atmosphere of his workplace. He'd switched from bartending to a job in a small workshop doing welding. He had been drinking too much at the bar. Now he didn't drink although he wished he did.

Simon purchased a bicycle in order to improve his stamina. It was a single speed with both a front and back brake. It didn't weigh much and Simon enjoyed coasting through the city streets. He didn't coast this close to the fight. He sprinted on his bicycle jamming the pedals down. His warm breath heaved into the night. His body began to warm up as the city cooled down with the dark of night.

By the time he got home the chill of the evening had dried the sweat on his skin. He shivered slightly when he went inside. He poured himself a glass of water and looked out the kitchen window of his apartment.

The city was buzzing with activity. The lights of the local houses were on, creating stagnant fireflies in the night. He could make out dark shadowy figures walking on the streets. The profiles of the pedestrians merged into the shadows of the buildings, and then the dark ghosts would dimly emerge only to be eclipsed again into the shade of the city structure. The city oozed, bled, and swallowed its inhabitants. Simon put his hand on the window. He pushed against the glass, testing its resistance. The city was much larger than his hand on the windowpane. He pushed against the glass pane again, warding the creature away.

•••

The car honked at him as he rode towards the gym. He moved over on the road. The car honked again, longer, louder. He pulled over and stopped. The car slowly passed him. Simon stuck his middle finger up at the passing car. The car pulled over. The driver got out. Simon put down his bike. The driver pushed Simon. The driver was taller and heavier than Simon, a white thirty-year-old. He postured and thrust out his chest, his chin, his attitude.

"What are you going to do bitch!?"

The driver pushed Simon.

"Why don't you get out of my way!? Get out of my fucking space!"

Simon let himself be pushed back. The driver came forward again, his arms in front of him. As the driver stepped forward Simon sent his left elbow into the bottom of the driver's chin. The driver's face blurred with motion. Simon exhaled with his strikes.

"I'm going to fuck you till you love me faggot."

The driver fell backwards. Simon punched the driver in the liver with a left uppercut to the body and then pushed him away. The driver stepped back a few feet and was attempting to solidify his ground when Simon leg-kicked him. The driver's leg crumpled as Simon's shin smashed into the driver's thigh. Simon pounced on the driver and sat on his chest. He began to rain down elbows on the driver's skull. The driver's face cracked open spilling out blood.

Simon stood up. He kicked the driver and took a deep breath. He went to the car and took the keys out of the ignition and threw them as far as he could away from the street. An older man was walking towards the car. Simon got onto his bicycle and rode away. When he was half a mile from the site he began to breathe regularly.

♦♦♦

Joe was in the gym locker room when Simon came in. He looked at Simon.

"What's up buddy? Hey you got some red shit on your elbow."

Simon walked into the bathroom and shut the door. He splashed some water on his face. He could hear the traffic roll by outside of the gym. The sound of the street filled his ears.

"You okay?"

Joe stood by the bathroom door.

"You're not puking up your guts to make weight, are you?"

"I'm cool. Just taking a dump."

Simon sat on the toilet for a few minutes and then washed his face again. He cleaned the blood off his elbow and came out of the bathroom.

Simon did pad work with Bryan. It was a few days before the fight.

Bryan stood in the center of the ring at the end of their last round.

"Remember you need to control the distance, you need to come in and chop that leg. Don't let him keep you at bay. Sometimes you're going to need to take one to give one. Now go hit the bag and knee spar with Joe for a little while."

Simon nodded and worked the bag. His elbow felt slightly sore, raw. His time at the gym blurred by like cars on the highway. He went home and showered.

♦♦♦

The next few days passed. He trained. The weigh-in day went by without event. The night before the fight Simon dreamt of flowers that bloomed after fires. He rose early and ate some oatmeal and waited for the hours to move along. Joe called. Simon picked up the phone.

"You ready? I am right outside."

"Yeah, one sec."

Simon walked out.

"Nice car."

"Thanks, you know how long I've been saving up for this."

Simon looked at the car. It was silver. The bumper was scratched but the car looked clean, just washed. It was from 2009, a gray sedan. The seats inside were leather. Simon got in. It was comfortable.

"I've been playing online poker for like four months and finally all those sit and go's paid off. You know I paid my rent with my poker expertise. I'm a gambling man, but really I play by the odds. You know?"

Simon sat in silence as they followed the highway to their destination. The pavement was smooth despite the lack of recent repairs. The state had been in a financial crisis for the last decade and infrastructure construction was always delayed. Meanwhile private construction within the city continued despite the recession. The city appeared on the horizon and swallowed the car up within its tall towers and narrow roads. The sunlight was blocked out by the height of the buildings. The only light that was cast down were rays reflected from skyscrapers' windows.

They arrived on time to the event, which meant they waited for an hour and a half before the pre-fight meeting was held. The promoter and the referees went over the rules. Simon was the third fight of the evening.

He began to warm up and changed. Bryan and Bee arrived a little late. Bee wrapped Simon's hands, lining them with a layer of tape, gauze, then more tape. An athletic commission official watched over them.

The first two fights passed quickly. Simon walked from the locker room to the ring. He followed Bee up the small stairs, avoiding the first step due to Bee's superstition. Bryan was close behind. The three stood for a moment on the ring apron. Bryan moved first.

"Go over the ropes. You come out the same way you go in."

Simon stepped over the ropes. He came to the center of the ring and graciously bowed. He made his way to the corner. Bee waved his hand at him and Simon began to walk around the ring with his hand on the top rope. He stopped at the corners and bowed down, sealing off the ring.

The ring measured twenty feet by twenty feet outside of the ropes. Inside it was sixteen by sixteen. The small size of the ring was used to make the fight more active. Simon felt the canvas beneath his feet as he walked. He breathed in and out with each step. He could hear Joe barking from the crowd.

His opponent entered the ring a few moments later. Simon didn't look up at him. He focused on his breath. The referee brought them together. He gave a few more instructions and pushed them apart. The fight began. The fight ended ten minutes later. Simon had judged the distance between the two and attacked, chopping at the taller man's leg. The taller man had his weight on his back foot when Simon threw his hand combinations. His opponent was unable to see the kick that cut at his leg. In the middle of the second round the opponent's lead leg fell like a tree cut down by a lumberjack. Simon threw up his hands in victory, pushing them higher than the skyscrapers outside of the venue.

•••

Joe stood by the door.

"You ready?"

Simon had changed back into his normal clothes and had watched the rest of the fights with Joe. Bryan and Bee had left already, having to work at the gym early in the morning. Joe walked out with Simon.

"Yeah."

The two walked to the car. Curbside lampposts lit the streets. They passed through patches of darkness into the parking lot.

"You did it, all that training paid off."

Simon got into the car and fastened his seatbelt. He put his hand on the dashboard.

"Thanks for all the help. I couldn't have done it without you, or Bryan, or Bee."

Simon took his hand off the dashboard and squeezed Joe's shoulder then let his hand fall back into his lap. Their bodies were close and highways apart. Joe pulled out of the lot and got on the onramp heading back to Simon's apartment. The city stretched out before them and behind them. The city sprawled for an eternity.

Butterbean's Belt

"Go talk to her, Simon."

We were at a bar in downtown. The lounge was close to the theatre and attracted a white-collar crowd. The brick-walled bar was crowded on the Saturday night. We'd arrived an hour or two earlier and had sat drinking some beers. Butterbean was trying to get me to talk about him to a girl, to play him up. The girl was attractive, a thin Asian woman with glasses. She wore a low cut dress and a locket that hung between her breasts. She was at the bar.

I walked from where we were seated on couches toward her.

"Hey, I like your glasses."

She turned to me. I made eye contact with her. She reciprocated.

"Thanks."

I groaned. I began my next line.

"How much does a polar bear weigh?"

I turned toward the bar, contemplating getting another drink.

"Uh…I don't know."

"Enough to break the ice, my name is Simon. What's yours?"

"Oh."

She laughed politely.

"My name is Jen."

She fiddled with her drink in front of her. It was some sort of blueberry concoction.

"How's your night going?"

"Oh, its okay, what about yours?"

"It's going great. I'm here with my friend. He's kind of a big deal. He's an ex-Muay Thai champion."

I pointed over to Butterbean. He was sitting straight up and attempted to casually wave. I swung my index finger in his direction. He was fidgeting with his fingers. I sighed quietly to myself.

"Are you here with anyone?"

"Um…"

She looked over to her right. She pointed toward a group of Asian girls.

"I'm with some friends."

"Well if you want to come over and sit with us that'd be great. My friend John, you know, the ex-champion, said he'd buy you a drink."

"Okay, yeah, maybe."

She fiddled more with her drink. The bartender came over and I got two more beers. I brought them over to Butterbean.

"So what happened?"

"She said she has a boyfriend."

"Figures."

"Yeah."

"I still think she was looking at me."
"Yeah dude, she was totally checking you out."

•••

Promoters in the fight game want excitement. To create that excitement they build fighters. Create a personality then market that personality. That's what sells tickets. Your average fight fan doesn't know much about the game, especially with Muay Thai still being a fringe sport here in the States. The fans can't always tell that the quality of a hook comes from the rotation of the core of the body. They won't know that a strong knee to the body is more disastrous to an adversary then a wide haymaker to the head. What they look for is someone who is busy in the ring, who looks like they have a good heart, and who wins the bouts.

Tony Stack, the promoter, came into the gym about four months ago. He watched some of the workouts and then came up and started to talk to Bryan. Bryan owned the gym and was the head trainer. He'd been to Thailand, fought out there, and had a decent career in the States. He'd fought for K-1, an international kickboxing promotion, a few times and decided to open his own gym.

The gym had only a few members when I joined. I'd noticed it when I had been walking to the park where I left Abby. When I looked into the water I didn't see her. The body had been washed away, or maybe it had decomposed. I left the park and joined the gym. I needed something.

Bryan didn't like Stack. Bryan claimed a moral stance when he said he didn't like promoters; he said it was what made him an ethical man. I could see him bristle when the short, stumpy promoter came up to the desk to talk to Bryan. They talked for a few minutes.

Stack smiled widely, giving Bryan a toothy grin. He wore a polo shirt, jeans, and heeled boots that made his short frame a few inches taller. The boots were freshly polished. Bryan sat back in his office chair, clad in normal gym apparel: Muay Thai shorts, a white T-shirt, and a pair of sandals.

Butterbean and I were knee sparring while they talked. We broke to take in some water. Butterbean leaned against the ropes looking at the men.

"What do you think they're talking about?"

"I don't know, probably match-ups. I hope I get a bout."

I'd been trying to move up in the ranks and things were slowly starting to come along. Bryan said that in a while I'd be a legit contender. He never gave me a timeline. "Soon," he would say. "Keep training," he would say.

We finished our knee sparring and did some sit-ups and push-ups. Butterbean groaned as he neared the last of his sit-ups.

"I'm so fucking tired."

"Shut up. You're almost done."

We finished. I walked over to Bryan. Butterbean showered.

"Did you get some match-ups for the next fight?"

I held my breath hoping that they'd discussed a title shot for myself.

"Yeah, you didn't get one. I'll have you fight on the next card. John, come over here."

Butterbean was zipping up his pants as he walked over to the gym desk, his hair was still wet from the shower.

"Listen, I might have a shot for you. It will be a close fight, but I think you can do it. You're going to have to train hard. The guy you're fighting is no joke."

Butterbean nodded. He never really cared about who he was fighting, he didn't really care too much for training. I hadn't been able to pin down what he really cared about. Everyday, Butterbean came to the gym. He trained with me. He'd fought a handful of bouts and had done pretty mediocre. Sometimes it seemed like his heart was in it but his body wouldn't respond, at other times during his fights his body acted accordingly but his heart was somewhere else.

"You've got four weeks. We'll start doing pad work tomorrow. What time can you come in?"

"I'm working during the day. I can come in the evening."

"All right. Well, come in after work. Start running. Have you been running?"

"A little, sometimes we go jog around the lake."

"Start running five or six times a week. If you can, before work."

"Yeah, okay."

Bryan told Butterbean the date of the fight and that he'd have to cut a few pounds. Butterbean, despite the lining of baby flub around his midsection, wouldn't have to cut that much.

"Simon, I want you coming in as well, I want you training with John the entire way. A good training partner is important."

"Yeah, sure."

•••

I drove my car home. My two-bedroom apartment was sparsely furnished. That's what happens when you have two working guys in a slightly overpriced neighborhood, I would always tell my rare visitors. I felt happy that the place wasn't decorated with empty beer cans, empty bottles of condiments, and pizza boxes with a few pieces of crust in them. I kept the apartment clean.

I went to the fridge and grabbed a beer. I tried real hard not to drink that much but even fighters need a break. I sat on my bed. It was the only thing to rest on in my bedroom. I pulled the tab and the beer hissed when it opened. It felt cold going down my throat. I drank it quickly then cracked another open. It was still chilly in my esophagus, it smothered the jealousy. My vision blurred on the edges.

I looked at the fight posters on my wall. I'd saved all of the posters from cards I'd fought on and cards I'd been to. I tried to go to all the local fights; it was a bit costly, not just in ticket price but from taking the day off work. A few of the posters had my portrait but I hadn't stepped into the ring. One fight, my opponent didn't make weight, which was ridiculous. He wasn't even within five pounds of the fight weight. Another fight, the bout fell through. Too many bouts on the card, the promoter had said. I got up from my bed and ran my hand down the posters. I sighed. I drank a final beer. Drunk and tired, I went to bed.

•••

Butterbean looked like shit after a week of training. He was a rag doll during knee sparring. His neck was a flimsy plastic flamingo. I watched him do pad work with Bryan. He would gas out after the second round. He wasn't bothering to do simple stuff like turning his hip over for kicking. When we would spar he wanted to counter, but he'd just wait there. When the round ended he said he was working on his defense. Bryan came over. He scowled.

"John, what the fuck are you doing? Do you want to fight?"

"Yeah I do."

"Well it doesn't fucking look like it. Where's your heart?"

"I got heart."

"I know but you're not showing it. You build your heart in the gym. It's in working through the pain and the annoyance of training. You're flopping around like you're a rag doll, a marionette puppet whose strings just got cut."

"Yeah, I know."

"Well what's your problem?"

"I don't know."

"Listen, this guy is tough. If you can beat him you'll get the belt. Maybe with that belt you'll get better fights, maybe we can get you into the professional circuit. Hell, maybe it will get you laid."

Butterbean muttered something inaudible and looked at Bryan.

"You decide John, I don't fucking care. You want this fight you have to train for it."

I looked over at Butterbean. He seemed weighed down with thought. It was the first time I'd seen him so burdened with the weight of thinking. He looked like a gloved copy of the Greek statue "The Thinker," contemplating the core of his motivation.

Bryan left the ring and went to sit at the desk. He began doing paperwork.

"Do your sit-ups, push-ups and pull-ups and go home!"

I nodded at Bryan. We took off our gloves and shin pads. I motioned for Butterbean to lie down. I sat on his legs so he could do Thai-style sit-ups. With each sit-up he would come up from a prone position, crunch down, and lie back down. He did one hundred. He looked at me.

"You think people care about belts?"

"Everyone wants one, right?"

"Yeah…I guess so. You think that girls would like it?"

I laughed. I remembered a boxing book I'd read.

"Girls love a champ. Like Mike Tyson. Dude was fucking so many girls that he lost fights. Like the night he had his bout with Buster Douglas in Tokyo. Tyson was banging so many hoes he didn't have any gas left in him and so Buster, the complete dog, won the bout."

I continued to chuckle. Butterbean seemed to be lost in thought. We did push-ups and pull-ups together then changed. Butterbean left without saying much.

•••

A few days later Butterbean was back in the gym. He was grave with determination. His eyes were fixed with intent. I'd never seen him look so focused. He pushed himself hard, and then harder. I didn't recognize him at all. While his technical skills didn't ascend to new heights, his attacks were much more dynamic and explosive. The lead-up to the fight rolled along quickly and I served as his sparring partner along the way.

The fight was set according to modified amateur Muay Thai rules: There'd be no elbows, no knees to the head, and the clinch would be broken up quickly. The fight would be quick, two minutes per round, with a total of five rounds making up the belt bout. The fight was held in an old high school gym. The crowd slowly filled up the bleachers. I took a seat and waited for Butterbean to be called up to the ring. He ended up being the last fight of the night.

The announcer cried out Butterbean's name and I saw him enter the ring. Bryan followed behind him. Butterbean was clad in a black and white robe with the gym's logo on the back. On his head he wore a *mongkol*. His opponent entered after him. His foe was tall and lanky compared to the shorter and stockier Butterbean. He gazed into the distance when the two fighters came together. The referee gave instructions. Butterbean looked beyond his opponent.

The fight began with a gasp from the audience as the two went to war. Most fights at the amateur level are trumped up brawls, while the more advanced ones are displays of technique with flurries of activity. Rare is it that you see an all-out war. Butterbean came forward into the center of the ring, marking the territory as his, when the bell rang he didn't just walk, he marched forward. His opponent threw two quick *teeps* into Butterbean's stomach. The push-kicks didn't faze Butterbean. He kept his chin down and threw a jab. His opponent backed up to the ropes and covered up. Butterbean threw a left hook into the uncovered portion of the body and then slammed a right cross straight into his foe's face, ignoring his opponent's guard. His opponent peeked out of his fists with concern. He circled to the side and threw a leg kick into Butterbean's thigh.

Butterbean continued his march. The other boxer pushed Butterbean off of him and threw a knee into

Butterbean's chest. Butterbean ignored the sound and sensation of the patella striking his core in order to jab then cross the face of his opponent. The bell rang. Butterbean went to his corner and sat down on a small red stool. Bryan talked to him excitedly. I could see from Bryan's motions that he was excited. Butterbean might win. The second round started and Butterbean trudged forward without grace. His adversary threw a left uppercut into his chin but Butterbean was unphased. In retaliation Butterbean threw a straight cross into his body followed by a flimsy leg kick. The taller fighter looked worried.

Butterbean stepped forward and his opponent threw an elbow. It slammed into Butterbean's temple and blood started to ooze down. Butterbean threw an elbow in return, his face looked annoyed with the break in the rules. The referee caught my friend's illegal technique but not that of the other boxer. I shook my head. Red liquid started to pour quickly down the side of Butterbean's face. I was worried that they might stop the fight. The bell rang for a second time.

Bryan cleaned Butterbean off and put a thick gob of Vaseline on Butterbean's face and then waved at the other corner, yelling at them not to elbow. He sent out Butterbean with a sip of water and a slap on the back. Butterbean had a few moments until the third round. I could tell by the amount of blood gushing from his wound that he would have to end the fight in order to not be halted by a doctor's stoppage. Butterbean used his hands as if they were hammers. He pounded into his adversary's temple with two sequential left hooks and then jammed a right uppercut into the poor man's nose. Ten seconds into the third round his opponent went down. The ref counted him out as blood began to drip from Butterbean's head onto the canvas.

The crowd screamed with excitement. Bryan rushed out of his corner and picked up Butterbean, ignoring the blood that was leaking onto his shirt. Butterbean looked out with glee. His eyes had changed from resolve to relief. After the fight we all went out to a bar across the street from the venue along with some fight fans. Butterbean sported a small bandage on the side of his head. He sat dumbly on a stool as people congratulated him.

I watched Butterbean happily talking to a girl. She blushed as I overheard him talking about his job. Bryan took a seat next to me. He had a beer in his hand. He took a drink.

"I'm real surprised. I honestly didn't think he had it in him."

"I know, I don't know how he did it."

"Fuck, I just put him in there because Stack needed an opponent. Stack offered a belt shot for you if I was willing to give him a body. John's never been that much of a fighter, but I figured it might be good for him, maybe having the belt as a goal would bring something out in him. It really looks like it did."

He looked towards the window.

"I'm glad I put him in there, but maybe I should have believed in him more."

"Yeah."

I was excited to hear that Bryan had made the move for me to get a fight. It made me happy that I'd get a shot just like Butterbean soon.

•••

Butterbean called me every night the next week. The conversation was the same.

"Hey, let's go out."

"Nah, I got work tomorrow."

"Come on, celebrate with the champ. We'll get some tail. Girls love a champ. Look at Mike Tyson."

"Mike Tyson is also a convicted rapist."

"Let's go."

I acquiesced once and we went to a local bar. Butterbean wore his belt out. It was large and ungainly on his jeans. I sighed when I saw him. The bar was a local spot for hipsters. The girls wore form fitted pants with high waists. The boys had traditional barbershop haircuts. I was pretty sure everyone in the dive had an English or Art History degree. I shuddered. As soon as we ordered our drinks Butterbean walked up to a couple of girls that were chatting. I stood close to him with a beer in hand.

"Hey, my name is John, I'm a fucking champ."

I groaned. The girls looked confused.

"Is that a band?"

"Yeah I think it is a band, the Fucking Champs. They're okay."

The other girl turned towards her friend.

"Are you playing around here or something?"

"No, I mean I'm like a Muay Thai champ."

"Mai Thai? Isn't that some sort of fruity drink?"

"No way, its Spanish for very Thai. I know, I took Spanish for a semester in college, and Thai is a type of food."

The first girl turned back towards Butterbean.

"Really!? So you're a really good cook?"

She looked Butterbean up and down with disdain and surprise.

Butterbean slumped his shoulders.

"No, I'm a fighter. Aren't girls into fighters? I mean I'm a champ, a fighter."

Butterbean's voice went soft. The first girl touched her necklace.

"I don't know. I guess I'm not really your type. I'm more into designers."

"Designers?"

The girls turned away from him. I clasped his shoulders. We sat at the bar and drank in silence.

"I just can't fucking believe it, I just can't believe it. I thought girls love a fighter."

"Yeah I don't know. Listen, I gotta work in the morning. Let's get going."

Butterbean nodded and didn't bother finishing his drink.

•••

He went up for his first title defense. He fought the same opponent he took the belt from. While his chin was just as strong as in the first fight, Butterbean didn't move forward. He hardly moved at all. The fight went unanimously to the challenger. Stack was excited prior to the fight about the ticket sales but afterwards was disappointed with Butterbean. Bryan told me later that my shot was next. I was ecstatic. After the fight we went back to the bar. Butterbean sat by himself. Later he came over and sat next to me.

"Everyone likes a fighter, right Simon? I mean, girls, they love a guy that's got a belt right?"

"Yeah, everyone loves a champ. They love a winner."

The Grounds

The two boys sat next to each other, each pushing their small cars around in the sandbox. Bryan watched his son and Chandler as they played. He sat on a wooden bench a few yards away from the two five-year-olds. He stretched out his legs and let the light wind blow on his face. The sun warmed his body to a point that bordered on overheating. A cool breeze came and dropped his body's temperature slightly. He looked towards the blue sky. The clouds lazily passed through the air, changing form with each moment. Bryan had brought his small stereo to listen to as he watched the boys play. He turned the volume up.

Dash, his son, and Chandler got together nearly every week. Dash was the quieter boy, Chandler more talkative. Dash acted with a simplicity that Chandler often tried to emulate.

Bryan's favorite song by the New Holidays was beginning. He'd rediscovered the song after hearing a modern singer cover the Motown song.

◆◆◆

"Bryan, come here."

Robert, Bryan's uncle, turned on the record player.

"Now, I used to shadowbox to a record, sometimes the Four Tops, at other times the Supremes. You too young to know what the good stuff is but…but, you'll learn at some point. Now each song on these records is about three minutes. A round in a fight is three minutes, give or take. Sometimes the referee cuts a few seconds short doing a dilly or ah dallying, and some…sometimes a boxer spits out his mouthpiece to stall the fight. Either way the…the round is about three minutes. Now what I want you to do Bryan, Bryan, come here."

Robert waved his hand at Bryan.

Bryan stepped forward into the barn. The barn smelled like hay. It had been unused for a long time. A month ago Robert had opened the barn doors and started to air it out. The record player stood on a small crate. A batch of records sat next to it in another crate. A heavy bag swung from the rafters. Bryan saw a tattered pair of gloves lying by the record player. The gloves were worn brown leather. The curving knuckles of the gloves matched the color of straw. The stitching was coming loose.

"What I want you to do is to watch. You at the age now where you should be learning how…how to deal with conflict. You gotta learn how to stick up for yourself. Now you youngsters don't have, uh, ah verbose vernacular to resolve your disagreements, so end up speaking far too little words and sending out far too many blows. You just like that mercantilism, all crisis all the time. You understand?"

Bryan nodded his young head. Having just entered kindergarten in his small rural town his personal experience was limited. He had only recently learned refined ways of describing his sexual organs.

A wind blew through the barn. The breeze brought in the smell of turned autumn oak leaves. It was the smell of passing time. In a few months the leaves would be gone, mulched in the ground. As autumn's scent passed through Robert, he thought of the coming months. The hard, bitter winters, when the weather would get so cold that the trees would snap at night. For Robert, life was a forever winter, never to thaw. He felt a need to protect his young nephew from the cold, not the cold of nature, which could be dealt with, but from the arctic essence of humanity.

Robert stretched his arms. He threw them over his head and then opened his chest, spreading his limbs wide. Bryan watched silently.

"You watch…watch me for a few minutes and then we'll get to your lesson. Now I know that most of your playground altercations won't be much like an actual pugilistic encounter, but by training in the sweet…sweet science of fisticuffs you might just be able to slip your way out of a jam, or if not, well, at least you won't think you're made of glass anymore."

"Maybe So, Maybe No," by the New Holidays came on and Robert was seized by a spirit of action. His lanky body created a whirlwind of action as he moved about the barn floor. He shuffled forward, then backwards. He slipped invisible punches and returned fire with lightning quick combinations. His canvas shoes made soft swishing sounds while his mouth emitted quick sharp exhales with every blow to his hidden opponent.

The combination of the record player and Robert's body movements made a cacophonic melody in Bryan's ears. The harshness of the sounds gripped the boy. He began to see his uncle's blows land on his opponent. Bryan began to hear the sound of slapping skin as his uncle's gloved hands smashed into a now visible body. Instead of a barn floor, Bryan saw a ring, spotlighted, with a black-and-white clad referee attempting to orchestrate the action according to the rules of the sport. The auditorium was packed with screaming men, all leaning forward, emulating the young men in the ring. The punters were attempting not only to mimic the actors, but through imitation to pull strings on the performers.

Bryan stood motionless long after the song had ended, entranced by the image of the ring and the actors within it. The record player's needle scratched on the record, filling the barn with a throaty hum.

"My lungs aren't what they used to be. I ain't doing that much road…roadwork, in the traditional sense. I still do plenty of work on the road, being my daily enterprise of labor, but my endurance ain't what it used to be. No matter, though. I'm not here to engage in battle, I am here to help…help a young boy grow into…Bryan, Bryan."

He waved his hands in front of the Bryan.

"Uh, sorry, Uncle Robert."

Bryan's daydream was whisked away. He felt himself fall back into the present.

"You don't strike me as the dull sort, though you are given to drifting into the mind's nether region. Now, though, I need you to pay…pay attention for a moment."

He stood in front of his nephew with his hands in

front of him. He patted Bryan's arms and then set his bony hands on the boy's shoulders. He turned Bryan. The child looked expectantly at his uncle.

"Okay. Now what?"

"So your feet should be pointing at two o'clock. Your feet are parallel. Your body is turned to the right-hand side, as you will be an orthodox fighter, being right-handed. Imagine your body as if it was a blade...blade. You want the point facing your opponent, that left hand should be nice and high so you can poke your opponent with your jab..."

Bryan spent hours in the barn with his uncle, practicing the art of mimicry, attempting to shadow the older man.

•••

David sat crying in the sandbox. His small wood car sat broken before him. A few yards away stood Doug The Skunk. Doug was in the third grade but was built like he was in the fourth and towered over the younger kindergarten student.

Doug's father was a skinner. Living on the outskirts of town, the family set traps for skunks. Doug's father would skin the skunks in the house and then sell the furs to merchants in the city. The stink of the animals clung to Doug and his siblings, who were the bane of the local schools. Doug developed a sense of venom for the other children, which matched his odor. The small school housed kindergarten to twelfth grade in one building, and the younger children shared a common recess. When the lunch bell rang the youngest children were let out into the school grounds and the terrorism would begin. Doug became the schoolyard tyrant, feared partially for his size, partially for his stink, and partially for his bravado in shoving the other children around.

"Why are you crying?"

Bryan walked closer to the sandbox. David sobbed quietly. He pushed at the small wooden pieces in front of him.

"My car was broken."

"Oh."

He stood for a moment in silence.

"What happened? Did you drop it?"

"Yes…no."

"Oh."

"I was holding it and then Doug pushed me. I fell on the car and it broke. It cut my hand. See."

David held his hand out to Bryan. David's small palm was scratched; a few tears of blood congealed on his hand.

"If my Uncle Robert was here, he wouldn't let that happen."

"Is your uncle taller than Doug?"

"Yeah, he's seven feet tall."

"I think Doug is nine feet tall."

"Well, my uncle is stronger and he's a boxer."

"Really?"

"Yeah, he's fought a million times, in a million places. He even taught me how to fight."

His chest swelled with pride as he thought of his uncle teaching him the rules of the ropes in the barn. Bryan positioned his feet as his uncle had taught.

"You just gotta do this."

He put his hands up and pawed at the air. His small fists pushing particles of the air to the side with marshmallow force.

"Wow. Do you think that you could do that to Doug?"

Bryan stopped his pantomime and looked at David. A chilling foreboding swept through Bryan's young body.

"You can, you can." David eye's lit up. "You can, you can!"

His voice picked up both speed and volume. His eyes scanned the schoolyard and he pointed behind Bryan.

The smell of skunk assaulted Bryan's nose.

Doug stood before the two boys. The smell of rot fell out of his mouth.

"What are you doing?"

He stood at the edge of the sandbox with his hands akimbo. David fell behind Bryan. His face peeked over Bryan's shoulder.

"Bryan is a fighter. A boxer."

"So, so what?"

Eyes shifted. The other children in the yard turned their gazes onto the three boys.

Doug stepped into the sandbox. Lurching forward with juggernaut steps he pushed Bryan. Bryan rocked backwards. Bryan breathed in deeply. The stink of skunk, the earthy smell of the sand, and the odor of fear sat in his nostrils. He stuck out his left fist as if he was a knight with a lance and ran towards Doug. Bryan's small fist smashed into Doug's nose. Doug cried out in pain a moment after contact. His eyes watered, and a small tear of blood ran down from his nose.

Bryan's blue eyes became oceans. His vision blurred as salt water filled them. Bryan ran out of the sandbox in equal time to Doug's own retreating steps. David was left alone in the sandbox, save for a small drop of red from Doug's bloody nose.

♦♦♦

"Let me have it."

Chandler grabbed the small car from Dash's hand.

The song came to a close. Bryan's gaze fell back on the boys. Dash looked confused.

"Can I have it back?"

Chandler pushed the toy car around the sandbox.

"Please?"

"No."

"Oh."

Dash picked up a handful of sand and let it slip through his fingers. Chandler continued to push the car around, ignoring his playmate.

"Come on boys, it's time to go home."

The boys picked up their things and walked behind Bryan toward the car. Bryan dropped off Chandler at his house. Bryan watched as Chandler walked up to and opened the front door awkwardly, clutching the toy car in his hands.

"You have to stick up for yourself sometimes Dash."

He looked at his son in the back seat. Dash looked out the car window, watching Chandler's front door close.

Dash sat in silence. The car began to move and the two made their way home.

"But Dad, if I fight with people, they won't be my friends."

Ekkamai Station

The heat and humidity made Sam's skin sweat immediately; it was a warm wet blanket that stuck to him. While the skyscrapers of Bangkok attempted to punch through the heavy heat that hung on the marsh, the swampy atmosphere persisted.

The Ekkamai BTS stop was in eastern Bangkok, part of the new development of Sukhumwit Road, a hub of international businesses.

Sam stood on the edge of the platform, behind the yellow line, waiting. They'd walked to the station together, stopping to buy some fruit. She'd brought a change of clothes so that she didn't look like a whore. Sam had used a condom because she was one.

The train system had opened on December 5, 1999, the king's birthday. Every morning at eight and again in the evening at six, the loudspeakers of each station let out the national anthem, attesting to the Thai sense of nationality and fealty to the dying king.

The passengers belonged to the middle class, white-collar workers shuttling from their homes to their offices. The

BTS beat the traffic of the roads, yet the expense made it less accessible to the members of the underclass that lived streetside. The workers were well-dressed, college-educated women. Their high heels, clacking on the floor of the BTS, made them two inches taller for an average height of five foot four.

She stood at five foot three in her heels. Sam was six inches taller in his polished shoes. Their white shirts matched, but his white skin contrasted with her dark Isaan brown. Sam breathed into his hand, it stank from last night's booze. She smelled of skin lotion. They'd gotten dressed as the smog covering the sun let some light into his Ekkamai apartment. The light was so dim Sam could never tell if the sun was up, down, or if it was the moon still waning. He'd gone from the station to Soi Cowboy, further down Sukhumwit and into the heart of the city, where the international business prospered. Everything in Bangkok is trafficked, Sam thought.

She came up and started to chat him up. He had been rooted in his seat. She made him feel desirable. Sam assumed she thought he was wealthy since he was a white in Thailand. He paid the fine to take her out of the bar and into the evening. She'd stayed the night.

His small studio was normal for the residential Ekkamai area with the usual surrounding accouterments: 7-Elevens, a shopping mall, pad thai stands, motorbike taxis, fruit vendors, and a nearby magazine seller that had the daily edition of Muay Siam, the Muay Thai rag.

Every morning he would drink coffee in his chair—it was the most comfortable thing he could find. He had looked for a month for a good chair, some place to sit. The chair molded to his body, or he to it. He would watch as

Muay Thai boxers ran past him, a pack of young wolves. They seemed so full of decision. Their lithe, taut bodies, pounded against the cement when they ran past. The boys had been commuted to the capital to fight for pay, most of which they would send back home.

He'd come to Thailand on vacation. Indecision had kept him there. He came for a week, which turned into a month, which turned into a year. There was nothing for him at home, no career, no relationship, no family, no self-esteem. He was fat and balding. He'd ended up staying, staying like a stick in swampy mud. He didn't want to sit another seventeen hours on a plane to go to a dead-end job, in a dead-end place.

He'd gotten a job as a teacher.

He looked up at the sky. It was only smog. When the rainy season came, the station was like the rest of Bangkok, flooded. While cockroaches drowned in the streets, workers would use large squeegees to push the rain into the water-logged avenues. Cars hydroplaned along the roads while the train continued to glide across the rails, seemingly oblivious to the weather. The workers would halt their travel, idling about until the temperamental storms passed. He always felt bad for the cockroaches, drowning in the pools of sewage water, little Josef K.'s swept away into some unexplainable maze, while the whole world just watched, idling about.

She chatted with him, practicing her English. It was good, and British-accented, probably the result of going to an international language school. She pulled out her iPhone and began texting.

The train pulled up and he saw their reflection in the glistening side of the locomotive. She looked like a student, dressed in her uniform for early university classes. He looked red-eyed, jostled along life's trajectories too much. She was put together, she had showered and applied light makeup.

"You call me tonight, okay *na*."

He grunted. She'd been sweet to him.

The doors opened and air conditioning leaked out, cooling his skin. The train was packed with others going to work. They slipped into the crowd. Sam closed his eyes as they escaped the smothering heat and felt for a brief moment that he was free of the mud.

Sleeping in the Dark

The black of night chilled Dash. Winter was approaching and the light of fall was disappearing. The rays of summer had long since passed. The child lay in bed and tried to imagine the summer sun on his skin. The blankets offered no substitution.

Bryan stood at the light switch.

"Can you leave it on, Dad?"

"Why?"

"It's too dark."

"Do we have to go over this again?"

"What if something comes out of the darkness? What if that thing under my bed comes out? What if I have to go to the bathroom and can't see anything?"

Bryan sighed.

"Can't I have a nightlight again?"

"No, we talked about this."

"Where is the cat? I can't see him. What if he gets lost because it's dark? Are the lights on outside so he can find his way home?"

"Cats don't get lost in the dark. They can see in the dark."

"But I can't, Dad."

"No, you can't."

"What happens if it stays dark all night?"

"It doesn't."

"But what if it does?"

Bryan could hear the beginning of tears, part of the routine over the last few months.

"How old are you?"

"I'll be seven in three weeks."

"Seven is a big number. Don't you want to be a grown-up?"

"Yeah…"

"Well grown-ups sleep with the lights off, with no light."

"What about the people that work at night, can't I just stay up all night and sleep in the day?"

"Goodnight."

Bryan turned off the light.

Dash pulled up his covers, staring into the white sheets, hoping that they would give him light. The blankets were black as night.

He couldn't stop thinking about what lurked in the shadows, what was waiting for him to close his eyes and be blind to the world. Growing older meant living in darkness, he thought. He didn't fall asleep.

Rounds

YAAK THI NEUNG

"*Chok!*"

The fight started. Simon stepped forward. He kept his hands high and touched his red gloves with his opponent's. The smell of menthol permeated the air from boxing liniment. The yellow oil was slathered on the fighters prior to entering the ring. Simon could see Vaseline glisten on his opponent's face. Sweat gathered on top of the thick gel.

Simon could hardly feel his fingers. They were encased in a mold of tape and gauze and then by red gloves. The cast bent his fingers into a permanent fist.

His opponent was dark-skinned. "Isaan," Simon thought when he was kicked in the inner thigh. The kick wasn't sharp, but Simon felt it all the same, an introductory shot. Simon varied his forward movement, trying to alter his timing. Simon's opponent looked as if he was only eighteen. He had a lean upper body and large legs. His tanned calves looked disproportionate in comparison to his upper body.

Simon took a small step forward and to his left. He threw his right arm out as his leg came up in the air, his hip turned over when his kick reached its zenith. His shin smashed into the Thai's arm. The Thai smiled and then pulled his left leg into his body and then sprang it out. The ball of the Thai's foot pushed into Simon's stomach as if the Thai were pushing the gas pedal of a getaway car. Simon attempted to retain his stance as he stumbled backwards two steps. The push kick hadn't hurt but had stalled Simon's forward momentum.

The Thai dropped his hands to his waist and shook his body slightly. Simon shrugged his shoulders, attempting to loosen up, mimicking his opponent. The white man's left arm pawed forward, gauging distance, and then his leg came up and swung over. The Thai picked his leg up and blocked the kick with his arm. The combination of the arm and leg molded together looked like a gladiator's shield. Simon's mouth stayed clenched as words eeked out.

"I want this."

The Thai inched forward, moving like a caterpillar. His body moved to a rhythm of a song that was unsung in the large auditorium. There was little noise in the venue save for the conversation of the punters. Simon could hear the crowd when they yelled at him. He heard Hmii's voice.

"*Teep, teep.*"

Simon pulled his right leg up and pushed it towards the midsection of his opponent. His foe scooped his leg to the side with a half crescent push with his hand and retaliated by kicking Simon in the back.

The blow smarted but injured Simon's pride more

than his body. His face flushed with embarrassment. The Thai stared at him, his gloves bouncing up and down to the same rhythm as before.

Simon's next pawing jab connected as he stepped forward with it, bouncing off his back foot. The head of his opponent snapped back and Simon took the moment to slam another punch into the boxer's liver. The Thai retreated for a brief second and Simon considered his next blow. The Thai rotated his shoulder, throwing a large right hand that Simon just barely parried, feeling the glove brush his face. The Thai followed his miss with a left hook that hit Simon in the temple. A sharp pain split into Simon's skull. He could hear Hmii from the corner.

"Block, block."

Simon blinked. He felt the position of his feet. He stepped forward on the ball of his left foot and let his hip swing over. The kick landed clean on the Thai's arm. The Thai walked forward with his right leg in front and skewed a left knee into Simon's solar plexus. Simon let out a small grunt as he felt the patella strike his abdomen.

Simon brought his red-gloved right hand down onto the Thai's shoulder. He returned fire with a knee strike of his own, but no sound was made by the Thai. The two began to vie for position, each attempting to gain dominance in the standing grapple of the clinch.

The Thai withdrew his hand from their struggle and brought his elbow back. Simon felt something hard strike his head and bit down on his mouth piece.

The bell rang.

•••

Hippy Da Bar was located off of Khao San Road. The local restaurant had both outdoor and indoor seating. The patrons inside were given recycled air from an air conditioner, whereas the customers outside were given mosquito bites and fresh air. Simon sat on a small couch near the entrance, outside. The wall facing the backpacker's ghetto had a large white sheet blanketing its surface and a soccer game was being projected on it.

The coolness of the beer slid down his throat. Simon looked up. He couldn't see the stars here; they were obscured by the Bangkok pollution. He'd never paid much attention to the sky when he was at the camp outside of the city. He couldn't remember the last time he'd seen the moon.

The soccer game didn't interest him; he'd wanted to come somewhere quiet and away from the gaping eyes of the other *farang* in the area. His black eye and stitched face made him stick out in the crowd of travelers and he didn't want to be bothered to speak to any of them.

He felt the bottle become lighter and raised his hand.

A waiter dressed in jeans and a worn T-shirt came over and took the beer from the table. The worker's eyebrows raised. Simon nodded.

"Beer, *krap*."

The waiter replied with a nod and went off for another bottle.

Simon fished his wallet from the back of his pants. He planned on drinking the majority of his bout pay away, if not tonight, then the next night, if not tomorrow, then the night after. The compensation for his time in the ring, 2,000 *baht*, wasn't much to begin with. If he were Thai that might be something substantial, but he wasn't, and it was just drinking money.

He'd spent the day touring Bangkok. The large city was pleasant to visit, with a plethora of different restaurants and malls. It wasn't too bad, he thought, as long as you don't mind traffic and pollution.

He went to see a movie at Siam Paragon, a large mall in the center of the capital. He watched an action movie he'd seen in the States before he left. The price was low, and Simon loved to get popcorn. He'd bought two different types, tamarind-flavored and sweetened. His metabolism demanded constant attention and he felt as if he could eat forever and not become full. After the movie he wandered around the shopping area but found little of interest so he returned to his hostel on Khao San Road.

Before checking into the hostel he'd considered staying at the camp for the rest of the week until his plane left, but decided he'd seen enough of rural Thailand. A day after his fight he took a minivan to the city.

The minivan pulled into Victory Monument and Simon was anxious to get settled. He took a cab to Khao San and rented a room. The shared rooms were cheaper but he opted for his own space. He left his bag in the room went to Siam Paragon, and then to Hippy Da Bar.

The cold beer felt good in his mouth. He swished it around and swallowed. It was only his third beer, but he felt the impacts. He stared at his hand and flexed it. It opened slowly. He remembered sitting by the ring and watching his hand get wrapped. Hmii had repeatedly told him to open and close his hand as the layers of gauze and tape wrapped around his fingers.

He got up and stretched his leg. The soccer game was coming to a close. He walked out of the bar after paying his bill and quickly finishing his beer.

The tourist ghetto was crowded with visiting foreigners. They talked excitedly to each other, clad in beer singha, or beer chang shirts. Simon stopped and stared for a moment. He walked over to a pad thai stand. The vendor's cart was piled high with different types of noodles. Underneath the cart was a blue barrel containing gasoline.

"Pad thai."

The vendor dumped noodles onto the iron plate. The order took less than five minutes. The vendor dumped the food onto a foam tray and Simon walked away with it. He sat down on the curb and slowly ate his noodles. The passing foreigners seemed to get drunker with every moment. His stomach was filled. He walked into a 7-Eleven and bought a large bottle of beer. He stood by the pad thai vendor and drank his beer until he was almost too drunk to stand. He wobbled his way back to the hostel and passed out. His body didn't feel the pain of his injuries, it only felt the alcohol.

YAAK THI SEUNG

The bell rang.

"*Chok.*"

The referee dropped his hand between the fighters.

Simon walked forward. Simon whispered words that his opponent couldn't hear, in a language that he couldn't translate, but would still understand.

"I want this."

The stadium filled with the music of the *pi java*. The three-piece band made of the clarinet-like *pi java*, drums, and cymbals created a haunting atmosphere between the two fighters. The crashing cymbals created a cacophony in Simon's ears as the Thai threw a left hook that crashed into his temple. Simon had his head down and took the punch. His chin was clenched. He was unfazed. The cymbals kept crashing.

Simon glided forward, stepping with his lead foot and sliding the rear foot forward with him to keep his same strong stance as he approached his opponent. The Thai jabbed at Simon but he parried the questioning punch away with a small movement of his right hand. Simon kicked the Thai in his left rib; he was unable to block as his body was stretched out from the punch. The blow left a red mark on the Thai's dark skin.

The *pi java*, whose sound came from blowing on a palm reed, reminded Simon of a dying cat. He was confused for a moment as he conjured up the image of a cat lying by the side of the road. The sprawling roadkill in his mind collided with his present, both had a similar sinister violence to them.

The blow of Simon's shin had no visible impact on the Thai other than the red mark. The Thai stood his ground, slowly bobbing his hands up and down in time to the music of the live band.

The Thai's forward movement matched the sound of the drums. The steady beat drove him forward as if he was marching on a Siamese battlefield against the Burmese. The constant percussion of the drums was discordant with the pounding of Simon's heart, which rang in his ears. "Thump, thump, thump," was all Simon could hear as the blood in his veins surged with adrenaline, attempting to oxygenate his muscles.

Simon pushed forward, attempting to gain the center of the ring where the Thai stood guardian. He came with a jab and a cross followed by a long straight knee that curved at its end to hit the Thai in the stomach. While the blows landed, the Thai didn't move an inch and instead fell into the clinch with the foreigner.

The music began to pick up speed as the two fighters tangled in each other's arms. Simon switched his feet so that he was parallel to the Thai and wouldn't be thrown. The Thai grasped onto Simon's hand and with his other gloved hand took hold of the nape of Simon's neck. The Thai pulled down on the foreigner's head and yanked him to the side in the same motion. Simon fell forward, his body splayed open. The Thai skewered his knee into Simon's chest, landing just below the diaphragm.

Simon couldn't hear the music. It seemed as if time had stopped, frozen, and then it started again, but more quickly, as if the sands of time were flowing faster for having halted. He gasped for air and forced his way back to an upright position. The Thai stood there.

Simon stepped back and swung his right arm over the Thai's guard as if his elbow joint was an axe. The blade of his elbow smashed into the top of the Thai's forehead, shaking his hairline. The Thai's hair wobbled back and forth in its glued state, stuck together with Vaseline, like reeds in a swamp during a storm.

The Thai took a step forward and Simon felt a slash above his eyebrow. He felt liquid run down his face. He shook his head and saw red drops fly onto the dirty brown canvas.

The Thai took a step back as if to appraise his work. Simon stepped forward undaunted and felt the familiar push of the Thai's foot moving him backward. Simon scowled, then shrugged.

Simon kicked at the Thai and the Thai took a small step back, leaning away from the blow. He sprang forward once Simon's leg passed his center point and kicked Simon in the chest. Simon cursed himself for his impatience and lack of timing.

The bell rang.

•••

"*Gam mat.*" Hmii looked at him.
Hmii closed his open hand into a fist.
"*Gam mat.*"
Simon looked down at his open hand. He closed it. Hmii wrapped gauze across the back of his knuckles. The white medical gauze felt soft on his skin, a light airy layer compared to the tape that had been placed on his hand. A length of tape had been rolled and placed on the back of his knuckles, creating a ridge. Simon wondered if it was fair to have such a hard ridge on his fist. He had looked over and saw the other trainers doing the same for their fighters. The rolls of tape looked like joints. Simon wondered if Hmii smoked pot.

"*Bpeh,*"
Hmii closed his hand and then opened it.
"*Bpeh.*"
Simon opened his hand. Hmii finished wrapping his hands.

"*Dii mai?*"
Simon opened and closed his hands. They felt like casts. His hands were layers of gauze and tape. Hmii led him over to an official. The man in uniform marked his newly wrapped hands with a marker.

Hmii took a small cup from the table. The cup had three strings, which secured it on the wearer like a thong. Hmii pulled down Simon's trunks. The foreigner stood in his underwear. Hmii reached around and put the steel cup over Simon's dick. Simon held it in place as Hmii tied it around his waist and then secured the third string between his legs.

"*Dii mai?*"

Simon squatted. He nodded.

Hmii walked over and picked up a pair of gloves from a table. They were red and used. They looked as if they'd been worn, and worn, and worn. The stuffing was thin on the ten-ounce gloves. Simon was sure that they were only actually six ounces now.

Hmii stuffed Simon's hand into the right-hand glove. He pulled it up tight. The laces of the gloves were thin. Hmii turned Simon's hand palm up. He took the laces and wrapped them around Simon's wrist. The strings were tight.

The official came over and wrapped Simon's gloved hands in red tape.

Hmii took a red robe off a hook. He opened it and slipped it on Simon. The satin felt clingy on Simon's skin. It was dark red and worn from layers of sweat, boxing liniment, and Vaseline. The trainer put on a matching red vest.

Hmii took the *mongkol* off the same hook. It had been hanging above Simon's head. The *mongkol* was beige with a blue tail. The white had turned tan with wear.

The trainer held it together between his hands. Simon bowed his head. Hmii whispered and put it on Simon.

The two walked towards the ring. Hmii motioned

to Simon to sit down on a bench and wait for the fight to end. Simon watched the bout. The two fighters were both young and small.

Simon didn't want to think. He wanted it to be over. His leg was shaking, bouncing up and down. He could feel the cold cement on his feet.

The bout ended. The referee held up the blue fighter's hand in victory. The boxer bowed to the crowd. The fighters left the ring.

Hmii motioned Simon to follow him. The trainer went up the three stairs to the ring. Simon skipped the first step. Hmii held down the top rope. Simon went over, feeling the taut cord brush against his steel cup. He went to the red corner. Hmii stood there and pointed him to the center of the ring. Simon saw his opponent.

The band began to play the *wai khru ram muay* music. Simon stood in his corner watching his opponent perform the dance. The boxer walked around the ring and then to the center. He bowed and lunged, splaying his arms out wide. He got up and walked with rhythm to the middle of the ropes. He waved his arms up and down as if he was a bird in flight. He returned to the center of the ring and walked backwards to his corner, keeping Simon locked in his gaze.

The two boxers met in the middle of the ring. The referee said something in Thai. Simon nodded his head, pretending to understand. The referee patted Simon's groin, feeling his cup, and looked at his gloves quickly. He nodded. Simon went back to his corner. Hmii took the *mongkol* off his head with a prayer. He put in Simon's mouthpiece. The bell rang. The fight started.

YAAK THI SAAM

Simon's gloved hand reached out to touch his opponent's as the third round started. The Thai briefly touched his glove and then push-kicked him.

Simon shook his head and the Thai's grin widened.

Thailand was known as the Land of Smiles, but there were a variety of smiles with a plethora of meanings.

Simon walked forward.

The punters outside of the ring were becoming more agitated and excited by the fight. They screamed at the boxers in the ring. Attempting to conjure up the correct movement from the fighters they flung their arms, miming an attack.

A man with a dozen cellphones strapped to his chest talked hurriedly, announcing the changing odds of the bout along with the action in the ring itself.

"I can do this."

The band's music was becoming more frenzied as the boxers began to engage in combat. The Thai walked forward with a long left knee that struck Simon in the gut. Simon felt the Thai clinch the top of his head. Simon shrugged his shoulders up and looked for a moment as if he was a turtle. He warded off the Thai's gloves and struck back with a knee of his own. He opened his hips and swung his knee into the ribs of the Thai as if he was slamming a door.

The Thai pushed him off and kicked his arm. It was a distinctive point, no longer did the kicks smart, now they hurt. Simon realized that he wouldn't be able to take many more blows. The Thai kicked again. Simon stepped to the side and caught the kick. It was a race as the Thai attempted to turn his hip over and escape Simon's grip while Simon attempted to walk forward. Simon won the short skirmish and threw the Thai's leg away. He was able to capitalize on the Thai's exposed stance and kicked the back of his legs, sweeping him off balance. The Thai fell on his ass.

The Thai grinned again. The same smile.

"*Arai wa, farang uan wa*," the smile said.

Simon's face made no change, it remained blank and steady. He looked like a white wall before the dark-skinned Asian.

Simon walked forward on the brown, sweat-covered surface. The Thai stepped back with his left leg and smashed it into Simon's right arm. Simon's arm dropped slightly, absorbing most of the blow. The Thai slid his leg from the foreigner's arm onto his midsection, halting Simon from moving forward. The Thai balanced himself on one leg and smiled.

"*Arai wa*?!"

Simon punched at the Thai with no effect. He was stopped. The referee came over and broke up the pointless struggle.

Simon advanced when the referee threw down his hand. The Thai grabbed Simon's shoulder and used his momentum to pull him into his knee. He felt a rush of air emit from his body as the Thai's kneecap pushed into his stomach. Simon dropped his elbow onto the exiting knee, a trick Hmii had shown him some time ago. Simon looked into the dark brown-black eyes of the Thai and saw no expression. He pushed the left hand of his opponent over his shoulder. The tables had turned and the Thai was open for Simon's own knee. He struck.

The Thai felt his stomach sinking. He absorbed the blow and stood up, his feet square to the *farang*. He opened up his hips and swung his knee cap into Simon's ribs. Then he pulled Simon to the right and kneed him in the mid-section again as Simon attempted to regain his balance. Simon pushed his hips forward as soon as his equilibrium came back.

The Thai pushed Simon away from him and threw a left kick. Simon didn't see the blow coming. His right arm fell lower.

•••

They had arrived at the stadium at eight o'clock in the morning. Simon's eyes were still covered in sleep. He was exactly at weight on the small red scale at the gym when he woke up, which meant he couldn't eat until after the official weigh-in. He wished he were able to shit so that he could eat.

The stadium was the size of a high school auditorium. Its exterior was drab, weathered by the pollution of Bangkok. The insides were worn by use and lack of upkeep. Simon signed some papers that were given to him. The contracts were all in Thai and he had no idea if he was signing away his life or not. Perhaps he could get a lawyer from the States to renege all these contracts, he thought as his pen flew across the paper. He wanted to get the weigh-ins over so he could eat. He was hungry. He did not care for legalese.

A line of young men, barely past the age of boy-hood, sat waiting to be called. Simon took a seat on the ground next to the row of fighters. They quietly talked to each other, one by one being called up to check their weight.

Simon was called up after twenty minutes. His ass had grown cold sitting on the cement floor. Hmii motioned to him to take off his clothes. He disrobed and stood naked before the scale. The large device looked like a huge grandfather clock. Its numerical scale swayed when Simon took a step onto its platform.

"*Hook sip sii.*"

The official pointed at the scale.

Simon felt Hmii touch his arm and he stepped off the scale. He put his clothes back on and followed Hmii outside.

"*Gin mai?*"

Hmii pantomimed eating food.

Simon nodded and followed Hmii to a vendor's booth right outside of the stadium. Hmii ordered a few dishes and Simon began to eat.

"*Bpai, grap baan.*"

Hmii hailed a cab. Simon dozed in the taxi and when they arrived at the gym he went to bed. He slept for two hours and woke. He lay in his bed, staring at the ceiling.

Eventually he got up. He showered. He walked outside. Hmii was sitting on a bench talking on his phone. The other fighters were preparing to go jogging. They rubbed boxing liniment on their legs. The smell of menthol hit his nose.

He sat on the bench next to Hmii and watched the dark-skinned man chat on his phone. Hmii ignored his presence. Simon turned his attention to the fighters. They stood up and stretched then began to walk outside of the gym grounds. He saw them slowly recede from his view as they walked away. Hmii continued to talk on the phone.

The trainer looked at him.

"Gin mai?"

Simon shook his head. He wasn't hungry, he was bored. The constant training of the past weeks hadn't prepared him for this slow period. At this time he was usually training, not idly sitting around.

Simon got up and walked over to the ring. The canvas on the ring edge was covered in black dirt from fighters' feet. The center of the ring was stained pale brown from sweat and grime coming off the boxers' bodies. A small tub sat nearby to wash one's feet before entering the ring. Simon sunk his feet into it, feeling the cool water. He stepped out and onto a towel that served as a drying mat.

He pushed the top rope down and stepped over it. The rope pushed up on his crotch. He hoped that Hmii would be able to push the rope further down when he entered the ring.

He walked around the ring slowly. The canvas flooring felt firm under his feet. His steps left small imprints. He stepped forward with his right leg and threw a left knee at his invisible opponent. He looked down and saw the impression of the ball of his foot on the canvas. It stayed on the mat for a minute and then the canvas resumed its original shape.

Simon sat on the ring's edge with the tight ropes in front of him. He lay down on the canvas. The ceiling of the gym was made of tin. When it rained the gym resounded with the sound of droplets hitting the roof. There was no rain today. Simon wondered when it would rain again.

YAAK THI SII

The bell rang.

"Again," Simon thought. Three more bells. This bell

didn't count. It was the bell at the end of this round that counted. Then the beginning of the next round. Then the final bell. Three more bells. Simon walked forward. He touched gloves with the Thai.

Simon saw that smile. That grin again. His stomach felt a push. That grin. Simon's abdomen was bent inwards by the Thai's *teep*. His attempt to gain ground was lost again.

I can do this, I can do this.

Simon's looping thoughts were stalling him.

Where was the progress, he thought. He had trained. He had trained so much. I can do this, he thought.

Simon jabbed. He threw a right kick. It landed.

Progress, he thought, the slow march forward.

The Thai stepped forward and kicked him. The blow landed on Simon's left arm. It hurt. The Thai kicked again, and the pain accumulated. Simon's arm began to lower, weakened by the attack.

He looked at the boy's shorts. They were glittery and blue. A script ran across them. It was an incomprehensible cursive. The distraction cost Simon a moment and he received a knee in the stomach.

The Thai clinched him. Simon felt the leather of the glove on the back of his neck. It pulled him downward. Simon scrunched up his shoulders. He tried to slip his arm around his opponent's neck.

The boy stepped back from their close engagement. He caught Simon's eye. Simon looked at him for a moment and saw the Thai take an extra step backwards. The Thai swung his elbow over Simon's arm. It cut across his head, sliding on the Vaseline. Simon felt his nose move slightly back and forth, swaying like a willow tree in the wind.

The Thai appraised his work and shrugged, then smiled.

Simon punched him. He followed the cross with an elbow of his own. The Thai took the punch but was able to evade the elbow. The boy stepped back.

The Thai smiled. He threw a left kick. Simon's arm sank more. He tried to jab at his opponent. The punch waned back to his shoulder as if it was a crescent in the night sky.

The moments passed, a slow passage of time. The bell rang.

Simon sighed. Hmii was motioning him to sit down. The stool sat on a round tin of metal. Water slushed around on the tin as Hmii poured more water on Simon. He pulled out his shorts and dumped water into his lap. Simon felt the cool water on his groin.

"*Dte! Dte!*"

He poured water into Simon's mouth. He swung his arm into the air.

The water dripped off his body and hit the tin like rain on a roof.

"*Peh laew! Peh laew!*"

Hmii was wet with desperation. Simon shook his head, not recognizing what the man said to him.

Hmii stood up straight and raised his arms over his head. He took a deep breath in.

"Same, same, same, same!"

Simon nodded. He wondered why he had come; it hurt.

Simon looked across the ring. The Thai boy was sprawled on his stool. He was listening to his trainer with intent. The bell rang.

"One more," Simon thought.

Hmii shoved the gumshield into Simon's open mouth.

"*Peh laew, dte! Dte!*"

He slapped Simon on the ass.

The referee brought the two contestants together. They touched gloves.

The music began again. It filled the spectators' ears. The *pi java* whined.

"I can do this."

Simon felt his opponent's glove.

•••

"You want to fight?"

Simon had been at the gym for two days.

"Yes," he said.

He'd come to fight. It was a long way from home but he was doing it. He was training in Thailand. He bowed to Hmii with a *wai*.

Hmii looked at him quizzically.

"Okay you fight, one week, two week."

"Yes."

He made his face look stoic. He would fight. It was meant to be, he thought. He imagined himself going back to the gym. Bryan would ask him how it went.

"I won, I went to Thailand, I fought a Thai, I won."

Bryan would nod with understated appreciation. Simon would begin his workout and watch himself shadowbox in the mirror. His reflection was of a warrior, not a boy, his movements would be those of a veteran of battle.

Hmii called him over two days later after the training session was done.

"You fight one week, okay *mai*?"

"Okay. Fight."

Hmii nodded his head.

Simon didn't sleep well that night. The room seemed excessively hot. The air conditioner seemed like it hardly worked. He wished he'd bought a fan. His roommate began to snore on the other side of the two-bed room. The room was laid out like a cheap motel. The two beds, an economical desk, a sink, and a bathroom. The toilet was in the same room as the shower. Next to the throne was a hose to spray your ass with. It had taken Simon a week to get used to the spray. The shower was never hot. Simon didn't care, considering the intolerable heat of the outside world.

He got up from his bed and washed his face in the sink. The water dripped down his brow. He could hear its light smack on the sink. He looked at himself in the mirror.

"This is it."

He woke up several times that night. He was lying in his bed when he heard Hmii knock on the door.

"Jogging, jogging."

His roommate snored away. Despite coming halfway across the world to train his roommate never got up in the mornings. He only worked out lazily in the afternoon. Most of his time was spent in bed or eating junk food from the nearby 7-Eleven.

Simon got up out of bed and put on his Muay Thai shorts. He stepped outside of his room. He shut the door softly. His running shoes were just outside the door. He slipped them on.

The Thai boys were seated on the edge of the ring

wiping sleep off their faces. They wore soccer shorts. They all loved Manchester United. The boys rubbed boxing liniment on their calves and thighs. The smell of menthol filled Simon's nose. A rooster crowed in the distance. The boys lazily stood up, one then another, until finally all were standing. They walked out of the gym grounds and onto the road. The pace was slow. One of the older boys began to jog. The others followed suit.

The daily run went down the main road for about one kilometer then followed a *khlong*. The channel of water was enclosed by cement. The water was brown and filled with refuse. Occasional clumps of green ivy filled the waterway. The plants were motionless on the water.

The sun began to rise. Simon looked directly at it. The star was a pinkish orange. It didn't burn his eyes when his pupils met it. The sun moved slowly in the sky.

There weren't many other people on the road this early. At times a motorbike with a sleepy-looking driver would speed past the boys. Simon kept his eyes on the horizon. He had read an article in a men's fitness magazine that it was good for your running posture to keep your eyes on the distance. The Thai boys' eyes wandered around the landscape. They talked to each other occasionally. Their soft voices broke the regular cadence of their shoes hitting the pavement.

Simon marked their run's progress by the landmarks that caught his eye. They were coming up on the final checkpoint already. A large pile of spirit houses lay next to the road. The houses were in various states of decomposition. A few had their roofs still while others had their walls broken. Large chunks of cement surrounded the mound. Simon wondered who had left them there. They looked like they had been there for a long time, damaged and ruined.

YAAK THI HAA

The bell rang. Simon stepped out. "One more," he thought, "I can do this."

The Thai boy smiled and threw a left kick. Simon didn't block. He saw a flash of movement, then it was dark.

His eyes opened slowly. He was lurching on the ground. His hands were splayed out before him holding his torso up. He swung back and forth like a pendulum. His ears rang like a clock tower bell.

"... *saam, sii, haa...*," the referee counted.

Simon pushed himself up. The ring's floor felt unsteady as if he was on a boat in a turbulent ocean. The referee kept counting. Simon staggered forward. The referee waved his arm in front of the foreigner's face.

Hmii was suddenly before him. He dumped water on his head. Hmii put his arm around him and brought him to the ropes. He pushed down the middle rope for Simon and ushered him through. He held his arm as he walked down the stairs.

Hmii walked with him to the back room. The other fighters looked at Simon for a moment then returned their gazes to the distance. Hmii sat Simon down on a bench and took off his gloves. Simon looked down at the gloves. His head was still spinning. The white castings of his hand wraps were browned with sweat. Water dripped down his head. Hmii shoved a water bottle in his face and made him stand up. He pulled down Simon's shorts and undid the thong of Simon's cup. For the first time since Simon started fighting he felt some relief. The steel cup dropped, clanging on the cement ground.

Hmii walked off. Simon's shorts were still around his ankles. His opponent came over and said something in Thai to him. He gave him a small *wai* and walked off. A garland of flowers hung around the winner's neck.

Simon pulled up his shorts and sat back down on the bench. His head still hurt.

Hmii appeared.

"*Ab nam, ab nam.*"

Hmii pointed to the bathroom and gave Simon his bag. He staggered to the bathroom. The bathroom had a few stalls with squat toilets and two stalls with garbage cans with a hose in them. Simon walked into the shower stall and shut the door. He turned the faucet knob. Cold water rushed out. Simon watched as the can filled. A bowl floated to the surface. Simon took off his shorts and stood in his underwear. His arm hurt. A drop of red appeared on his chest. He took a bowl of water and dumped it over his head. It was cold. He shook his head. His hair clung together from the Vaseline.

Simon toweled off and went back to the dressing room. Hmii was sitting waiting for him. The Thai man grabbed his face and bent his head over.

"*Maa, maa.*"

Hmii grabbed Simon's hand. The trainer went to a back room and opened a door. A Thai man sat on a chair before a long waist-high table. Hmii talked to him rapidly and then motioned for Simon to lay down on the table.

Simon thought the man might be a doctor. The Thai man swiped his forehead with peroxide. It bubbled and burned. Simon winced with pain. His face felt swollen. The doctor swiped a local anesthetic roughly around Simon's cut then began to sew Simon shut. He pinched Simon's skin together. The needle felt sharp in Simon's skin and he could feel the thread as the doctor worked through the gash. He was given ten stitches. Simon counted them in the reflection of the bathroom mirror after they were done.

Hmii took his hand.

"Okay, go, go home."

Simon nodded his head dumbly, wondering if he had heard the last bell or not. He winced as he stepped outside of the stadium. His head rang.

•••

The airplane that would take him to Thailand taxied to the boarding gate. Simon could see it from his seat by the terminal window. The large beer sat in front of him, half empty. He moved the beer around the table. It made his fingers wet. He wiped them on his pants. The beer slid down his throat. The next beer was larger and cost more. Food was expensive at the airport, not that he could eat anyways.

"Just don't come back a ladyboy." Bryan had been sitting at his desk at the gym. His sandal hung lazily off his foot. "I know you can get a cheap, grade-A vagina there but really it might not be the best investment. Think it over before you get it."

Bryan had smiled for a long time and waved Simon out the door. Bee had been asking him for a week when he was going to leave for Thailand, as if he couldn't ever remember the date of the departure.

Simon had saved enough time off at his job for five weeks vacation. He scoured the Internet for two weeks and bought a ticket online for a reasonable rate. His budget was set and secure. The southeast Asian country was cheap, the currency exchange rate was high. Everything was going his way. Why did he feel so nervous then, he thought.

He remembered when he went to Mexico. He'd crossed the border filled with alcohol. The border police didn't stop him on the way down or on the way back, despite his less-than-coherent driving. He'd traveled internationally before, why did it matter so much this time?

He tried to imagine a glorious return. The boys, his coworkers, the guys from the gym, waiting for him at the bar, sitting there expectantly with an extra beer, colder and better tasting than the one set before him.

"I just came back from Thailand. Whores, booze, and I beat up a Thai. I trained relentlessly. My bout was difficult but nothing I couldn't handle."

The beer was getting warm as he drank it. The lobby was full of Asians, more than he'd seen since he went to Chinatown on a lunch date with a girl. She was an accountant. They'd met at a bar near his work during happy hour. She wasn't Asian but thought that Chinatown was quaint, "novel" was the word she used. She worked near him. They didn't make it past the electricity of happy hour to a subsequent dinner date. The emotions fell short.

Across from his seat in the terminal was a couple. They were old, Simon couldn't tell how old, but well past their prime. They chatted with each other in their language. Simon could hear it faintly over his iPhone. He was jealous with their familiarity. He worried that his phone battery would die during the flight. The plane ride was long.

He imagined the exotic jungles of Thailand, just outside the airport; the taxi ride that would bring him through the swampy marsh of Bangkok to the Muay Thai camp. There would be a heavy bag, a ring, and other boxers.

"Boarding for flight from San Francisco to Thailand, now seating rows A1 to B15."

Simon downed the rest of his beer. He wobbled to a stand and queued up with the other passengers. He pulled his ticket out of his pocket. It shook in his hands. The line took ten minutes. He followed the others. The old Asian couple hobbled forward. They seemed to take forever. He wanted to get by them to get to his seat. The flight would take fifteen hours, then a five-hour layover in Beijing.

The seats were lined with polyester. The cushioning thin, but plain. The old Asian couple was seated across from him. They chatted quickly together. They were still in Simon's way when he went to put his bag in the overhead compartment. He had chosen the aisle seat. The two people seated next to him came in late.

He turned up the volume on his iPhone. The music filled his ears, overcoming the noise of the passengers. He could still hear the chatter of the stewardesses explaining preflight instructions. The plane began to taxi on the runway. The alcohol was wearing off. He wanted another drink. He closed his eyes. He daydreamed of the glories of his return. He looked at his phone, he wanted to text someone. He couldn't think of anyone. He turned off his phone. The plane accelerated.

"I want this."

A Fighter Without Significance

I looked at the glass in front of me; my hand reached out and grasped it. It was wet and cold on my fingers. I brought it up to my lips and drank from it. I set it down and looked at the open book before me. The stories, they'd calm me, distract me, not let me think of the fights. I started needing to suspend my thoughts. My mind had been running in circles. The tread of my mind was gone, burned out from endless cycling.

The first few Muay Thai fights I lost I attributed to negligence. Like every other artist, I was reluctant to accept the evidence of my disintegration. I thought I was not taking my opponents seriously enough. I buckled down, I trained harder, I focused, I watched tapes, I listened and memorized the words of my trainer like a Christian memorizing Biblical passages. I attributed my losses to bad decisions. I knew that my old self, that self that didn't seem so distant, would have won the last few fights without a doubt. American judges are biased with their fixation on boxing instead of clean knees, elbows, and kicks, I would cry. It was with those thoughts that I took on a last minute bout. It was against an up-and-comer named Greene.

Greene was a young black man. The announcers said he was athletic as he stepped into the ring. Barrel-chested with skinny legs, he fought with his fists and not with his head. If the fight went my way, if I performed well enough, I would get another bout. If not, my career would bottom out on me. The chair would be kicked away and I'd be hanging from the noose. I'd have to go back to doing tiling jobs with my uncle to pay the bills, or bartending instead of fighting regularly.

I began the first round tempered. I opened up with a few jabs that were meant to distract and annoy rather than to convey force. I was nodding to the judges as I threw out my punches.

"I can play by your rules and still win," my movements said.

I kicked Greene hard in the arm with my left shin that he failed to block. As I slid back from his shorter frame he came forward whipping his arms left and right, and his fists smashed into my head. My skull was shaken; it was a feeling I'd often had, the headache, the disorientation, the stars, and the struggle for recovering. I blinked and backed away. He came in pushing me towards the ropes and threw a simple jab-cross combination. The cross caught me and I fell to the floor. I bounced back up, wanting to show that this old heart still ticked. I'd been downed before and gotten back up to win the bout. I laughed to show my courage. I stepped forward and leg kicked him. He blocked but we both damaged our shinbones. He sunk his chin into his chest and came forward. I push kicked him off of me and the bell ended the round.

It's always been funny to me, the passage of time in bouts. It is slow, gel-like, and incredibly fast. The mind works in fragments, thoughts aren't completed, actions are performed instantaneously, the body moves without consciousness. My mind didn't reflect on philosophies while on the stool in the corner, they reflected on the simple act of breathing. I hoped that a simple steady breath would clear my clouded head. Bryan thought differently. He jabbered at me excitedly to keep my hands higher and to quit walking into punches. I tried to focus on what he said, but the words were garbled. It was hard for me to focus both on breathing and his words.

When the bell rang opening up the second of the five rounds I took a final conscious breath. Greene opened up the round with a hard low kick to my leg. Not suspecting this sudden change in attack, I ate the kick. I could feel the damage on my thigh. A long nerve runs down the outside of the leg; if kicked repeatedly, the leg will go numb, the fighter will topple over, his frame undermined. I kept my hands high and kicked at his arms. I hit him twice in a row in his left arm. My hopes were to damage his arms, to tire them so that they'd drop or lose enough steam to no longer deal more punishing punches to my aching cranium.

Watching the tape later I saw the ending blows, but I didn't see them then, in the ring. I was up against the ropes, having backed away from my smaller opponent. At some point I'd forgotten to circle out and had instead moved straight back into the ropes. I reached forward to clinch Greene but he shrugged off my attempts to grasp his neck. In that moment he found leverage to throw two hooks, one coming from the left which hit my arm, the other coming just a second later and connecting with my jaw. I crumbled to the ground. I woke up a minute later. The fight was over.

That was two months ago. Bryan still said he was looking for more matches for me, but I knew that I'd sung my last song. If any more bouts came my way they would just be parts to play. I would be just another opponent. I continued to go to the gym. I exercised and worked with the other fighters as if nothing had happened, but something had.

"What are you reading?"

I looked up from my empty gaze at the novel and turned to my left. A young Asian woman sat next to me. Her face was round, her skin white, and her frame petite. She was sitting apprehensively on her stool, her shoulders turned toward me, her legs crossed and tucked under the bar. It was a little dark in the bar where we met. I liked it because of its near proximity to my own residence, close enough to stumble home from.

"Oh…uh, it's Raymond Carver."

There was trouble on my tongue. My disturbance came from my slight intoxication and the break in my train of thought. It was hard for me to switch gears.

"Which one, is it *Where I'm Calling From*?"

"No, it's *What We Talk About…*"

"I've never read that one. How is it?"

"I like it. It's terse."

"Will you read me some of it?"

She looked at me expectantly. I sighed and began the last few pages of the first short story but paused after only a few sentences.

"Why did you stop? Are you tired? I'll read the rest to you. It sounded pretty good."

She read the rest of the story to me. I bought her a

drink, thanking her. After finishing the story we talked about books we liked. I told her about the time I went and saw "No Exit." She said that she had wanted to go but couldn't find anyone to go with. After last call and the lights were turned on in the bar she asked me if I wanted to go back to her place and have another drink. She lived in an apartment not far from the bar. She opened a beer for me when we got to her place. I sipped a little bit of it. She moved towards me. She pulled off my shirt. She traced her finger over my tattoo of Sam. We had sex.

The sun rose.

"Did you love your dog?"

"Of course."

"Was it sad when she died?"

"Yeah."

"I had a dog once. I was inside my house. I was just a little girl. I heard a screech then my dog yelping. I went outside. The dog was bleeding. The car had driven off. The next door neighbor had come over and was next to the dog.

"'It's okay,' she had said. 'It's okay.'"

She got up. She poured me a glass of orange juice. I sat up in bed.

"So what do you do for a living?"

"I do office work for a tech startup. What about you?"

I thought about lying to her. I thought about telling her about my last bout. I thought about telling her I was a bartender again. That I worked in a welding shop. That I was, am, a professional fighter.

"I'm in between jobs right now."

"Oh. Want to go get some coffee?"

"Sure."

Acknowledgements

I would like to thank my trainers, Coke Chunhawat, Ganyao Arunleunt and Mike Regnier, and Bruce Sherrod for introducing me to the sport along with guiding me along the way. A hearty thanks goes to the various gyms I've trained and fought out of: Ingram, Fighting Spirit, Pacific Ring Sports, and Sitmonchai.

This novel wouldn't have been possible without the help and encouragement of Brad Andalman, Jonathan Bardelline, Kaitlyn Entel, Lee Hunter, Brad Lambert, and Jirayut Saosuwan.

Thank you to all the various people that have gone unmentioned as well.

About the Author

Born in Cobleskill, New York, Matt Lucas moved to the Bay Area in 2004 where he began to train in Muay Thai. He is a veteran of Rajadamnern Stadium in Bangkok along with other locations in Thailand and the United States. He currently trains at Pacific Ring Sports under Ganyao Arunleung and Mike Regnier. He resides in Oakland California. *The Boxer's Soliloquy* is his first novel. More of his writing can be seen at www.mymuaythai.com and at www.matt-lucas.com

CPSIA information can be obtained
at www.ICGtesting.com
Printed in the USA
BVHW041936210920
589301BV00016B/648